Jesus Lopez

Patria
or
Death

Printed in the United States of America.

First United States Paperback Printing: December 2006

ISBN# 978-0-6151-3725-4

10 9 8 7 6 5 4 3 2 1

"Patria or Death," a tale of caution.

No world event occurring right now has more impact on South Florida than the health of Cuba's leader Fidel Castro. But while most of Miami is preparing for a celebration, there is also a danger that should not be overlooked.

During my research for this story, I spent countless hours reading about the leader and the man, Fidel Castro.

This extremely intelligent man has escaped numerous attempts on his life and his regime. He has matched wits with US Presidents and often ridiculed them by his actions. We still remember the Mariel boatlift.

How would a man that scared Nikita Khrushchev during the Cuban missile crisis by saying that he and his country were ready to die for the cause, act when he knows that his days are numbered? How would he like to be remembered in history?

During my research I found a caption from one of his letters that date back to the beginning of his revolution, "I've sworn that the Americans are going to pay dearly for what they are doing. When this war is over a much wider and bigger war will begin for me, the war I am going to wage against them."

In a recent speech, he mentioned that letter and those same words.

Yes, the man could be dead as you read this, and these words would be as obsolete as the novel I wrote. Believe it or not; I could only hope, however...

What would a dictator do when both his health and his power are slowly slipping away?

Two things have been a constant aggravation:

1. The United States never truly left the island, making their presence in Guantanamo a constant reminder of this.

2. The Cubans that left the island arrived in a new country and made a home so close. How could he die when the driving force of all his hatred resides less than 100 miles away?

What would a man a Dictator, blinded for so long by his believes do when he knows that his life is coming to an end? Would he die peacefully in his sleep or would he continue his fight until his last dying breath?

After all, what does he have to lose?

This is the story; a story that I hope will never come to pass.

To my sons Kristopher and Michael, may you both continue to meet each challenge with the determination and the drive you've always shown me. You've made me the proudest father and even prouder to say I look up to you both.

And to my wife, Ily for always encouraging me to be myself; even when it means putting up with my craziness. I love the thought of growing old with you.

Prologue

============

The ocean lashed out furiously at the hull of the Coast Guard Cutter Manitou. The 110' Island Class Cutter remained motionless unaware of the waves reaching out like hands trying to reclaim what was taken away from it so suddenly. The crew, also unaware of the ocean's plead, worked furiously trying to bring the precious cargo aboard.

Captain Ronald Haas watched the crew as they brought a second body aboard the cutter, a young woman, that like the man before her, was found dead in the make shift raft floating aimlessly.

Haas was a guest aboard *Manitou*, a friendly gesture from the Lieutenant in command, allowing an ex-commander aboard his old ship once more. The Captain spent the first few hours moving about the ship, walking through the old familiar deck that he called home for so long. Even the first call brought back memories, as *Manitou* raced to intercept another migrant raft close to the beaches of Miami. What they discovered however was slightly different than anything he remembered.

Lieutenant George Williams remained silent as the second body was brought on board. As the Commanding Officer of the CGC Manitou, Williams had seen his share of migrants, none ever looked like this.

Turning around, Williams met his Executive Officer who was walking in his direction.

"What do you have for me Jones?" he asked not waiting for Jones to fully arrive.

"It's not good sir," Jones replied. "*Dolphin* is requesting a status, they might require assistant."

Williams acknowledge his XO's statement. "We'll be underway as soon as we bring the raft aboard. Make sure we're ready."

Lieutenant Jones turned and walked away, leaving Williams alone once more.

Since leaving port, *Manitou* was monitoring *Dolphin's* situation. A 31-foot boat overcrowded with Haitian migrants tried to outrun the Coast Guard Cutter, only to begin taking water and was now close to capsizing.

Manitou was heading to aid *Dolphin* when they were diverted to their current location, a routine pick-up that turned into something much different.

"Not quite what you expected for your cruise?" Haas asked Williams.

"Sorry Captain," Lt. Williams said. "I was hoping to provide you with a more enjoyable cruise."

"What do you have?"

"Is strange, first of all, this location is wrong; the currents would've never brought them this far. They were probably dropped off near here; by someone."

"Kind of far from shore," Haas commented.

"Probably got scared and ran when they were seen." Williams' eyes remained watching his men, who continued to work on bringing the raft on board. "Another weird thing, there were only two people in the raft. That's very unusual."

Haas nodded.

"And still, what bothers me the most is the bodies. The woman had multiple stab wounds, while the man had a single shot to the head."

"Strange," Haas added. "Why would they be carrying that type of weapons on the raft?"

"We found the knife, the man was still holding it, but there's no trace of the gun."

Ensign Matthew was moving slowly away from the body of the woman being carried away. He remained with her as she was taken on board, his hand still holding on to hers, as if trying to help her.

Gradually, he began to let go and walked away from her, not noticing the voices around him.

His mind was not registering the blood covering part of his uniform, nor the small cylindrical tube he was holding in his right hand. Matthew could not feel his feet moving, drawing him closer to the two senior officers nearby. His mind continued to see the face of the woman; gasping for one last breath before she died in his arms.

He reached the two officers and stood there, not fully realizing where he was.

"Matthew? Are you okay?" Williams said turning to face him.

Matthew's eyes were glazed and Williams' voice did not seem to reach him.

"Blood!" he finally said. "So much blood."

"He's in shock," Haas added.

Williams signaled for Jones to return. Lt. Jones, who was now approaching them, realized immediately what Williams was trying to tell him.

A tear began to roll from Matthew's eye as the man continued. "She was alive," he whispered.

"Are you sure about this?" Williams asked softly.

Jones drew closer to the young Ensign, walking behind him not to be seen.

"She was alive! She wanted me to contact the Captain. She said she needed to talk to the CIA."

Lieutenant Jones moved closer and put his hand on the young Ensign's shoulder. "Come on son, you had a rough day."

"NO!" he shouted. "She gave me this!" Matthew's right arm was now extended, his hand open showing the small tube in his hand.

Captain Haas was the first one to react. "Could I see that son?" he said with a gentle voice.

Matthew handed the Captain the tube almost immediately. "She told me not to open it. She said that it was important."

The captain remained silent, slowly examining the tube.

"Isn't that one of those metal cigar holder?" Jones asked.

Williams nodded slightly, noticing the look in the Captain's eyes. "Sir, is everything okay?"

Haas said nothing at first then raising his eyes back at the young Ensign he asked him. "Who else knows about this?"

"No one sir." Matthew answered. "She told me to talk only to the Captain or the CIA."

"Yes, you said that already," Lt. Jones interrupted.

Captain Haas looked at Jones, his hand motioning for the man to back up slightly. Once again he turned back to Matthew. "Son, you need to keep this between us; at least until we return." His eyes watched Matthew carefully. "Do you understand?"

Matthew nodded slightly.

Haas turned to face Lt. Williams, ready to give him an order and stopped himself. "I think we have a problem."

"Sir?" Williams asked.

"Oh, hell!" Haas complained, looking directly at Williams. "Son, I hate to do this to you but I have to. God knows how much I hated it when it was done to me." He turned to Lt. Jones, his voice now harsh and strong. "Jones, have the kid checked by the doctor, but he must not leave your side. After that, keep him in a secure location, you may want to use any private quarters you can find."

Jones eyes darted between the Captain and his Commanding Officer, trying to get some kind of an answer from Lt. Williams. He found none.

Haas did not wait for a reply, turning immediately to Lt. Williams. "Contact *Dolphin,* tell them we have an urgent situation. Unless they seriously need our assistance, we will be returning to port."

"Yes sir," Williams said immediately. "May I ask—?"

"We'll talk about it after we find out *Dolphin's* status." Haas turned his attention at the seamen raising the raft. "Get that damn raft onboard now!"

Chapter 1

==============

The soothing island breeze moved a page of the newspaper he was reading. He let the paper drop slightly to feel the breeze on his face. He loved to feel the breeze on his face, remembering ages ago when even the wind was against him in the unforgiving mountains.

Breakfast was now his favorite time of the day. It was the only time he was not too busy attending countless tasks and chores. This was the only time that he could rest, as most of the island still slept, unaware of the day ahead.

He closed his eyes, as he did every morning, to hear the noises around him. There was a slight rustling in the bushes nearby. His bearded face hid the smile as he pictured the large iguana moving cautiously from its hideout. The iguana was now his only companion in the morning, moving slowly but sure, waiting for the piece of fruit he would throw at it as he did every morning. In return, he would wait quietly, listening for the slight hint of movement opening his eyes when the fruit, like a projectile, would hit the large reptile on its head.

The morning air was crisp, with a slight breeze moving from the ocean, carrying the sounds further. Once again he closed his eyes, trying to listen to the ocean, not far away. It was the perfect morning for it; he could almost hear the waves, clashing against the sand, in a constant struggle, not unlike his life.

The sounds of shoes behind him made him realize that his peace was all but vanished.

"Have you seen this?" the visitor asked tossing a copy of the *New York Times* on the table, nearly spilling the coffee. The old man, his eyes once again fixed on his newspaper, paid no attention.

"I mean—"

"Shhh!"

The visitor sat down immediately, waiting for his brother to finish.

The old, bearded man folded the newspaper and placed it gently on the table.

"*Miami Herald*, why do you bother with that garbage?" Raul Castro asked, knowing too well that he would receive no answer. He was wrong.

"Because." his brother said. "This is the best way to know my enemy better."

Fidel Castro seemed unusually peaceful this morning, something that startled his brother. "So, what's the problem?"

Raul began immediately. "There's an article in the *New York Times* that I think you should read."

"Regarding Alvarez's death I presume."

"In a way," the younger brother said. "Jose Marcano is demanding for the American authorities to find the murderer and hand him over to us."

"Right," Fidel answered reaching for the *Times*. "Alvarez was a fool walking the streets of New York without a bodyguard."

Raul nodded in agreement as if trying to impress his brother. "But what about Marcano, he should've waited for you to make the announcement. If you ask me I think he is becoming a little too powerful."

"Only in his own mind mi hermano. Marcano is an idiot." Fidel stood up, knowing that any chance of a quiet breakfast was now gone. He tugged his uniform's shirt down and stood up straight, as if the entire island was watching him. "Still, his followers are growing, and I think he's becoming a threat to us."

Raul nodded.

"Whatever Alvarez was doing for Marcano is no longer important, since he became another statistic of crime."

"I do have to admit, that was one expensive hot dog," Raul replied trying to hide his amusement.

Fidel did not smile back at his brother; his mind was already planning his next move. "Did you bring me the list?" he said finally.

"Yes." Raul handed him an envelope. The older brother opened it and began to read the names on the list.

"Are you sure these people are to be trusted?"

"Absolutely. I personally removed anyone with ties to Marcano. I also got rid of a few people with questionable records."

Fidel eyed the list once again. "It is getting shorter."

"Mi hermano, I know we've dealt with people like Marcano in the past. He is not the first one; he will not be the last."

Fidel put the paper down and looked at his brother. *He's so old!* He thought, looking at his face, his wrinkles. *We're both so old!*

"But Marcano has charisma; he has gathered many followers in so little time." Raul continued.

Fidel nodded in agreement. "And he has contacted the Americans as well."

"No!" Raul shouted. "When?"

"I will know soon enough, but Marcano's ambition is growing too rapidly." Fidel moved around the table, his finger tapping the copy of the *Miami Herald* newspaper. "You are right about Marcano; he is not the first one we've dealt with in the past. Unfortunately people like him continue to appear, and as you've shown me in your list, we're losing followers."

"So we're going through with this?" Raul asked.

"Everything has been in place for over a year, but we will have to make some corrections." Castro sat back down, for a second he looked like the old man he truly was. "I think we don't have much choice." Fidel said. "Can we meet our original date?"

"Command has been in place since March, although they have no details."

"Good! Let's start mobilizing as soon as we get more information on the American satellites."

"Already working on it," Raul remarked. "I also have Maldonado working on our other little problem."

"Great." Castro paused for a second.

To Raul his mind was working furiously on another idea. It was a look he knew well.

"Have Maldonado pick the remaining 'spies,' even if they are only suspects. I think I found the perfect way to get rid of Marcano and all his friends."

Chapter 2

===============

Steven Conner gunned the engine and the sports car responded immediately. It had been only a few hours since he arrived in Miami but Conner was feeling at home once again.

He grew up in this city, spending most of his youth in a neighborhood not far from his current location. Leaving for college, Conner did not return to Miami until years later, only to leave once again for good.

His job took him around the globe, visiting exotic locations and meeting countless of interesting people. Working for the CIA had his advantages. For Conner however, his heart always remained here. That was the reason he was here.

Conner could not pass up the chance of visiting the city. A small, unofficial job with little importance, but Conner immediately requested the task. He wanted to visit his old city once more, but there was something else. For some strange reason during the briefing he sensed something, a small nagging feeling that urged him to be the one coming to Miami.

His first stop was at 'Exotic Cars Rentals,' where he picked a small, fast, convertible for his stay in Miami. After all what better car to drive in sunny South Florida than a convertible. The car was expensive but compared to the price he paid in other countries it was a steal. His second priority was food and Conner drove looking for some good, old-fashion Cuban restaurant.

Only then did he call the man he was here to see, Jerry Henderson. Henderson was in charge of the FBI's Cuban Affairs task force monitoring certain Cuban cells in Miami. He had also met Conner a few years back as their jobs brought both men together during an investigation of a South American Crime Lord.

Conner jotted down the address Henderson gave him and race to meet him. On the way he wondered if Henderson's current 'stake-out' was a coincidence or if Henderson was staging this for his benefit.

"Hey, Steven," Henderson said opening the door and immediately giving the visitor a hug.

Conner felt slightly uncomfortable but returned the hug. During the trip Conner remembered most things about Henderson. Short and balding, the fast-talking Henderson always looked like he was high on life. It was annoying at first, but once a man got to know him, Henderson was a man you could count on.

As the men walked in, Henderson looked apologetically, noticing the condition of the hotel room. "Sorry," he said glancing slightly at the man sitting by the row of monitors. "This is Angel Acosta, our AV expert."

Acosta waved his hand, his face hidden behind the trail of smoke from his cigarette.

Conner returned the wave, noticing that Acosta was once again concentrating on the video monitors in front of him.

Henderson hit him on the back. "I understand you guys are having a little problem down in Havana."

Conner raised an eyebrow but said nothing.

"Oh, come on Steven, it's not every day you guys come into our front door begging for help."

Conner faked a smile, still saying nothing. He knew Henderson was right, he was here because they needed help any kind of help and the window was slowly closing in. *Still*, he thought. *No sense in letting my guard down so easily.*

"Fine, fine," Henderson said. "Tell me what you can."

"About a week ago we lost communication with some of our top agents in the island. When we tried to investigate, we lost contact with others."

"You think there's some kind of a leak?" Henderson asked.

"Probably," Conner continued. "Problem is that every time we've contacted someone else, the person seems to vanish as well. As of yesterday, we've lost most communications with the island."

"Have you tried sending someone in?" Henderson asked.

"Didn't work." Conner answered abruptly.

"Bummer," Henderson added. "Meanwhile you have the Cubans creating a commotion in New York."

Conner did not tell Henderson that all communications with the island were now severed until more information was obtained. If the line of communication was compromised, as everyone feared, further attempts could only jeopardize those now in hiding.

Conner nodded.

"So how can we help?"

"Seriously, I don't know. All I know is that I'm here to spend a few days with your team; try to find out if there is anything happening here that might help us."

"That's pretty much all I know as well. I have a meeting scheduled for tomorrow at 10:00 AM in my office. You can meet the rest of my team then." Henderson moved behind Acosta. "The reason you guys are probably interested in our little operation here is probably because of this guy."

Conner walked around the table and stood beside him. As he drew closer the stench of smoke and sweat exuding from Acosta's body made Henderson look apologetically once again.

Acosta turned a switch and the speakers around the monitors came to life. "Great sound system, huh?" Acosta said louder than he should have.

Henderson pointed at the monitor labeled #2. "The man on the screen is Jose Gonzalez, who works for INS."

Conner seemed interested.

"This is a live picture from his apartment across the street." Acosta added.

"We took a certain interest in Gonzalez a few months ago when his name continued to appear during our investigation of the Carbonel case."

"Carbonel?" Conner asked trying to remember. "Oh, the migrant smuggling ring."

"Right," Henderson said. "It turns out that our friend Gonzalez was the man who processed most of the guys being brought in; not to mention all of Carbonel's men."

Conner was really interested. "So Gonzalez is playing for both teams?"

"Appears so," Henderson said. "Anyway, he got a strange call this morning and he immediately called in sick right after."

"Want something to drink?" Acosta asked his breath no better than his body odor. Conner shook his head.

A buzz through the speakers made everyone cringe.

"Sorry," Acosta said. He pressed a switch and three recorders began to process all the information being received. "Okay, here we go!"

"Buenas noche."

"Ignacio, adelante, adelante."

Henderson continued; his voice lowered to a whisper after a dirty look from Acosta.

"Gonzalez was watching his back for awhile, but lately he's gotten a little reckless, Cuban machismo and all."

Conner's cell phone rang and he excused himself as Henderson picked up another headphone to listen to the exchange across the street.

The sound of the speakers reverberated around the room forcing Conner to cover his other ear to hear better.

"Are you sure about this?" Conner asked. "Yes, I understand."

Conner finished his call and turned his attention back to Henderson; the look in his face, however, made Henderson ask.

"Everything okay?"

"Yeah," Conner lied.

"Listen up," Acosta broke in. "The visitor just mentioned something to Gonzalez about choosing sides."

"Choosing sides?" Henderson asked looking back at Conner. "What do you think he—?"

"It's your call Jerry." Conner said moving toward the door. "Something came up and I seriously have to go." Conner knew that Jerry Henderson was an intelligent man, his hunches often turning into good leads. "I'll give you a call in a couple of hours."

"Sure thing!" Henderson said picking the headphones again. "You know what Conner," he said holding the cord. "I don't care what they say; I like it when our agencies work together like this."

"You're just an old softie Jerry." Conner said closing the door.

Chapter 3

===============

Conner waited for the traffic light to turn green, allowing him to cross the one lane bridge into the Coast Guard Base. Beside him, a small group of Cubans stood near the entrance of the bridge with signs protesting the return of another group of Cuban migrants back to the island.

The light turned green and he crossed the bridge entering the base. A large guard was standing at the end of the bridge waving him to stop by his side.

"May I help you sir?" the guard asked.

"Yes," Conner said showing his identification. "I'm here to see Lieutenant Williams."

The guard looked at Conner's identification and pulled out a clipboard. "I need a driver's license as well sir."

Conner complied and the guard began to write the information.

"Here you are sir," the guard said returning Conner's license and a temporary visitor's parking pass. "Second building on the left; visitors' parking will be on the side of the building. Make sure the pass is clearly visible."

Conner drove away, making certain to follow the speed limit. He noticed the activity on his right as a crew loaded boxes into a Cutter. As he parked, a tall, lean, black man, wearing a Coast Guard uniformed began to move in his direction. Conner's eyes immediately scanned the man's nametag.

"Mr. Conner?"

"Lt. Jones," Conner replied stepping out of the car and extending his hand. Jones shook it. "You are the Executive Officer of the *Manitou*?"

"Yes, sir." Lieutenant Jones moved slightly ahead of Conner. "If you'd follow me, sir."

Conner immediately began to walk, hurrying his pace to catch up with the officer.

"According to my information there were two people on the raft."

"Yes sir. That alone was strange since the raft was big enough for at least six people."

Conner made a mental note as the man continued.

"Also, the location of the raft was all wrong."

"What do you mean?"

"Weather condition and currents, the raft should not have been in that position."

"You think they were dropped off?"

"Either that or they weren't meant to be found," Jones said without hesitation. Stopping next to the docked Cutter, Jones pointed at the gangway. "This way sir."

Conner walked up, stopping in front of a man that he knew was the Commanding Officer. "Permission to come aboard, sir."

"Granted," the man said with a slight hint of amusement.

I thought that was the protocol, Conner thought noticing the amusement in both officers' faces.

Jones was already by his side. "This is our Commanding Officer, Lieutenant George Williams."

"Welcome aboard CGC Manitou," Williams said.

"Thank you; Lieutenant Jones was filling me in on your find," Conner said keeping in pace with the other two men. "He said that the amount of people in the raft and the location was not the norm."

"No sir," Williams added. "The moment we reached the raft we were aware that something was wrong. Of course, the location and amount of people was nothing compared to the condition of the two passengers." Williams held a door open for Conner. "The woman had multiple stab wounds and the man had one single gunshot to the head." Williams continued.

"Someone else?" Conner asked.

"That's the strange thing. We found no other weapons but the knife, still in the man's hand." Williams drew an object from his pocket. "And of course there's the matter of this." He handed the small cylinder to Conner. "I believe this is the reason why you are here."

"Looks like a cigar tube," Conner said unimpressed.

"That was our assumption as well; however Captain Haas said that we should contact someone. I don't know who he called, but here you are."

Conner placed the tube in his pant's pocket and continued walking. "I was told that the woman was still alive."

"We don't know, Ensign Matthew said she was alive." Williams said.

"What do you know about the Ensign?"

"Ensign Matthew?" Williams asked. "He's a good kid...first cruise."

"Not a good way to start," Conner said.

"No, it's not." Jones opened the cabin door and the three men entered.

Conner noticed Ensign Matthew sitting in the corner; the worried look in his face was evident.

"Ensign Matthew?" Conner said shaking the young man's hand. "My name is Steven Conner, I'm with the FBI." He lied, knowing the officers would not contradict him.

Matthew seemed uncomfortable. "Am I in trouble?"

"No, not at all," Conner said sitting down on a chair next to Matthew. "I do need you to tell me exactly what happened."

Matthew remembered his face feeling rubbery, partly by the sun and the wind hitting his wet face. The salt had dried out and was making his arms and face feel as if they were tightening more and more.

"We arrived on the RHI."

Conner looked back at Lieutenant Williams.

"Rigid Hull Inflatable," Williams said. "We sometimes need to deploy it to avoid the raft being smashed by the Cutter's hull; this was one of those cases."

Conner turned back to the Ensign. "I'm sorry, please continue."

Matthew nodded. "Someone screamed for me to help the woman. At the time we didn't know they were dead." Matthew paused slightly. "Well, she was not dead...I mean not yet."

"I understand." Conner said.

He remembered stepping into the make shift raft, pieces of woods put together on top of three large truck tires. The floor felt slippery, at first Matthew thought it was due to the water but then he saw it. The sea had washed away most of it, but there was blood on the boards, and the woman. She was covered in blood.

"Holy Christ!"

He heard a voice behind him and turned to look as Seaman Bradley stepped slightly away from the man lying on the raft. Suddenly he felt a tug on his arm.

"She was alive!" Matthew cried out. "She grabbed my arm and asked for help."

She was barely alive, her breathing almost non-existent, her words almost a whisper.

"Ayudame," she whispered to him.

"So she spoke to you in Spanish?" Conner asked.

"No sir. Ayudame was the only word she said in Spanish. The rest was in English."

"Sorry," Conner said. "Please continue."

Matthew knew enough Spanish to realize that she was asking for help. "We're here, we'll help you," he said trying to comfort her knowing that she might not make it to the ship.

"CIA, need to talk to CIA," she whispered the pain written on her face.

"Bradley I need help!" Matthew yelled. "This one's alive." He turned to look for Bradley but he was helping another Seaman as they moved the body of the man into the RHI.

She grabbed him again, this time pulling Matthew down to her.

"Give to captain," she said handing him the small cylinder. Her voice seemed stronger; her grip was inescapable.

Matthew nodded. "I will, I promise."

"Don't open it," she almost shouted, her body arching back completely tense.

Please don't die! Please don't die! His mind continued to shout.

"Don't open it," she whispered as her body relaxed finally collapsing in his arms.

"Her last words were, not to open it." Matthew straightened himself on the chair, his eyes fixed on the cylinder Conner was now holding in front of him. "The way she said it, she made it sound important."

"Is this the cylinder?" Conner asked.

"Yes sir."

"Do you know what this is?"

"I believe so, sir. It looks like some kind of cigar tube."

"I think so too," Conner said working on the cap.

Matthew's eyes were even wider now; panic was setting in.

"Hmm," Conner said. "Yup, it is a cigar after all." He looked back at the two officers who seemed motionless. "You smoke Ensign?"

"No sir."

"That's good," Conner replied, his hand placing the cigar back in the tube. He read the label on the tube, turning his attention back to the kid. "*Cohiba*, arguably the best damn cigars in the world; unfortunately they're illegal in the U.S."

Ensign Matthew blinked.

"Are you okay?" Conner asked.

"Yes sir, thank you."

Conner stood up from the chair and moved closer to the kid. "I'm sorry, I know how you must feel." He kneeled down in front of the young Ensign. "Maybe she was trying to tell us something, but I guess we'll never know."

The kid nodded.

"Tell you what; I'll make some calls see if anyone can find something else. Maybe the actual tube means something to the CIA."

Matthew's face changed slightly; a hint of hope began to appear.

"You promised her you would help her. I promise you I'll make sure someone in the CIA hears it."

"Yes sir." The words almost escaped him.

Conner stood up again and began to walk away.

"Thank you sir." Matthew's face was looking brighter now.

Conner turned. "I do need a big favor from you; you must keep this to yourself. Whether something happened or not; there is no reason to bring this up again."

"I understand sir."

Conner nodded at the two officers.

"You're dismissed, Ensign Matthew." Lieutenant Jones said.

The young man got up and moved rapidly across the cabin and through the door.

Lt. Williams closed the door once again. "I suppose you want to make arrangements for the bodies."

Conner noticed Williams' eyes were still on the cigar tube he was holding. "Yes, sir. I'll make arrangement with the local FBI office to have them picked up."

"Understood, the release forms will be ready."

"Thank you." He pointed at the phone on the desk. "If I may."

"Of course," Williams said stepping aside.

Conner picked up the phone and dialed Henderson's number. After providing him with the information he hung up and turned to Williams. "Could we step outside?"

As the men walked outside, a tall, older man joined them.

"Captain Haas? My name is Steven Conner."

"Nice to meet you," Haas said shaking Conner's hand.

Lt. Williams' eyes were still on the cigar tube Conner was holding. "Mr. Conner, could I please take a look?"

"Sure," Conner said handing Williams the tube. "You can have it."

"No sir, thank you. I don't smoke." Williams replied. "Was this the same tube?"

Conner was about to respond but Haas interrupted. "If I recall correctly, the label said '*Cobiha*,' this one says '*Cohiba*'."

Conner smiled back at the Captain as Williams returned the tube. Immediately, he handed the tube to Captain Haas. "Even if you're not a smoker, try it."

"I have. Damn good cigars."

Conner nodded in agreement.

"1983," Haas said, his body turned slightly as an invitation for the two officers to join them.

Lieutenant Williams realized the gesture and moved closer. "I'm sorry sir, I don't think I understand."

"Early fall of 1983; we picked up a raft near Key Largo with twelve people on board. As we began to bring them onboard, a young man requested a meeting. He said that his life was in danger. The man handed me a tube just like this one." Haas tapped the tube as the men continued to listen. "Well, it was a different tube, with the name *Cobiha* instead of *Cohiba*. I remember that I didn't notice the difference until we reached port."

Lt. Jones' eyes were now fixed on the tube, trying to read the label. Haas noticed the man but ignored him.

"I remembered his words. He said that the tube needed to reach someone in the CIA and that under no circumstance it should be opened."

"So what happened?" Conner asked.

Haas continued. "We made a few calls and both the man and the tube were taken away. A week or so later, Marines landed in Granada and stopped a Cuban invasion on that island." Haas walked closer to Conner still tapping the tube of Cohiba.

"I know the rules Mr. Conner. I also know that something happened out there and I know that she was trying to communicate something to us." Haas returned the tube back to Conner. "May I please ask you a question?"

"I'll try to answer it if I can."

"My question is did we waste your time?"

Conner paused slightly and handed the cigar back to the captain. "Enjoy the Cohiba, Captain." He turned to each of the men and shook hands once again.

"Gentlemen, it's been a pleasure."

Williams noticed the smile on Haas' face, as Conner walked away. "Apparently we didn't."

Chapter 4

================

Conner returned to his hotel room after a quick stop to a local drug store.

Placing the small bag on the table, he began to open the shades to allow more light to enter the room. The view overlooking the ocean was impressive, something that Conner missed when he first arrived. Now, after opening the shades, he realized how amazing the view was.

With enough light coming into the room, Conner moved the table closer to the bay window and sat down. He opened the bag and removed a packet of pins and a small magnifying glass. Opening the packet he removed two pins, placing the packet on the side of the table.

Conner took the cigar tube from his pocket and placed it on the table. There was no difference between this tube and the one he gave to Captain Haas, except for the name printed on the tube.

Placing his thumb and forefinger around the cap, he attempted to unscrew it, applying very little pressure to the cap. As he expected the cap did not budge. He knew that using enough force would open the cap; he also knew that it would also destroy the content inside the tube.

Conner picked up the magnifying glass and began to search through the tube carefully. As he scanned the fine print, he immediately noticed a small indentation, hidden as the dot of the first 'i.'

Conner placed the first pin on the dot, pressing slightly until the dot gave in, allowing the pin to penetrate into the tube. The procedure wasn't delicate but he needed to make sure not to push too hard or else the pin might puncture one of two small gel packets hidden inside the tube. If either packet were release, the content of the tube would be destroyed immediately.

Conner felt the pin stop as it reached the other side of the tube.

He turned the tube slightly, finding the second perforation, hidden as a '.' at the end of the fine print. Again he duplicated the procedure, moving the pin all the way into the tube until it stopped.

Conner wrapped his hand around the tube, holding it for a few seconds, feeling for any temperature change. If the gel packets were punctured, the chemicals inside would overheat, creating a reaction that would destroy all content inside, while making the outside of the tube extremely hot, burning anyone that touched it.

Knowing that the content was safe, he twisted the cap, using the same amount of pressure as before. The cap began to open immediately.

The tube was now obsolete due to the easy access to telecommunication equipment, but in the past it was used to transport microfilms and other sensitive materials. Even on the island, it had become the easiest and safest way to move information without being detected.

The content was a disappointment immediately, as a small strip of paper dropped to the table.

Conner unrolled the paper to find a few quick words scribbled on it.

FECHAS DE LA REVOLUCION
CARTA – 5 DE JUNIO, 1958
GUANTANAMO EN PELIGRO

Conner pulled a pad and began to write, replacing the Spanish words with English ones.

Living in South Florida for so many years had its advantages, some became useful in his line of work. Being fluent in Spanish was definitely one of them.

Conner put the cap on the tube and closed it. When he left the Coast Guard base, he thought the content would answer some questions; instead it only created more.

The ring of his cellular phone startled him.

"Conner," he said to the receiver.

Steven, it's Jerry the voice on the other end said. *I just wanted to let you know that we should have a preliminary report on the two bodies by tomorrow's meeting.*

"Thanks, Jerry," Conner replied

That's not why I called. Jose Gonzalez is dead.

Conner had to think for a second before he recognized the name. "What happened?"

Our visitor returned again, it practically caught us by surprise. Gonzalez was not expecting him but let him in nevertheless. Anyway, in less than a minute, the man shot him and escaped.

Acosta was alone and by the time he realized it, the man was gone.

"Do you have any idea who he is?"

No, but we're still checking. We did a complete search for prints and got absolutely nothing. We're checking all our databases right now for anything.

"Keep me posted."

There was a small pause before Henderson continued. *This is just too weird. I mean what happened to Gonzalez and the bodies we picked up for you. I think something's going on Steven.*

"So do I Jerry," Conner said.

Conner hung up the phone and immediately dialed a number. The voice of a woman announced that she was not available. He tried her cell phone number and received a message as well.

Dialing back her office number, he waited for the machine to pick up one more time.

"Ann, it's Conner." He noticed his voice sounded dry and cleared his throat. "The tube was in fact one of ours. Found a paper inside with some words scribbled. The first line mentions something about 'dates of the revolution.' I need you to find an expert on Cuban history, specifically Castro's Revolution. I also need to know anything special about June 5, 1958. Letters, special notes, speeches, anything like that."

Conner paused slightly before continuing. "The last reference has me a little worried; it says that Guantanamo is in danger. Unless there's something else we are not aware of, I think they are referring to our Naval Base in Cuba.

Call me at my cell as soon as you get something." He paused trying to find something else to say but couldn't.

Hanging up, he walked to the window and stood there, watching the ocean, looking so inviting.

"Hell," he said. "I'm in Miami; there's nothing else for me to do today."

Chapter 5

========================

"Jose!" The voice shouted from across the room.

"Tomas," Jose Marcano waved back as the man approached him. "What are you doing here?"

"I don't know. The old man sent me a message that he wanted to meet us."

"He flew you in all the way from Washington? Must be something important."

"I heard he is making some kind of announcement," Rogelio Gutierrez said.

"You're here too? This must be important," Tomas Fernandez said hugging the new arrival."

"Maybe he will give you his blessing Jose, maybe he's finally stepping down." Gutierrez joked.

"Hardly," Marcano droned back. "I think he will die before he gives up his power."

"That's not what I heard," a new man joined them.

"Felipe!" Fernandez shouted hugging him as well.

"Hello Felipe," Marcano said dryly. "What do you mean by that?"

"Rumor has it that he is going to announce a successor, and it won't be his brother."

"What? How do you know this?" Fernandez asked

"I overheard Colonel Guerra. He is his latest confidant isn't he?"

Two of the men nodded

"I believe he will be choosing you as the new President of Cuba," Felipe Perez said looking directly at Marcano. "Of course I'm sure he will be staying as some kind of advisor."

"Of course," Fernandez said sarcastically.

Marcano remained silent. He was thrilled to hear the news, the fact that he was finally going to achieve what he had wanted for so long. He could not believe however that Fidel Castro would relinquish his power to him. True, Marcano had become very popular, even among the people, but he never suspected that he would gain control of the island without some kind of a struggle.

"Felipe!" another voice joined the group.

"Juan Carlos, how are you?" the two men hugged. "I'm so sorry about your brother."

The other men mumbled something in unison.

"Thank you gentlemen. It seemed that it was fate." Juan Carlos Alvarez said.

"What's being done? Have you heard anything?" Fernandez asked.

"Nothing, according to the authorities, it was a random violent crime."

"Where was his bodyguard?"

"He left him behind; at least that's what the bodyguard said. To be honest I believe him, my brother hated to be followed around like that." Alvarez turned to Marcano. "By the way, thank you for your concern. I read what you said to the Times."

"No problem, it's the least I could do."

"Hey," Fernandez whispered getting the men's attention. "Isn't that General Alarcon?"

"It appears we're going to have a full house today gentlemen." Gutierrez commented.

"This means, we'll be here all night." Fernandez added.

Gutierrez face turned serious. "Well I hope he makes it brief, I have a date tomorrow night."

The men all began to laugh.

"Here they come," Fernandez announced.

The doors opened wide as one of the servants moved into the room and asked everyone to sit. As they did, a dark looking man, wearing an expensive Italian suit walked in and sat on a chair in the corner of the room.

"That's Domingo Maldonado, the new Head of Intelligence." Perez whispered.

"We know," Gutierrez whispered back.

Fidel walked into the room followed by his brother, two steps behind. Although his step was much slower due to his age, Fidel Castro still commanded a presence as he walked.

Everyone stood up in attention as he reached the large table and sat down. With a hand motion everyone sat in unison. Raul stayed standing at his brother side, not like a bodyguard but rather like a trained attack dog.

"Good evening gentlemen, I guess you are all wondering why I asked you here today."

A few 'yes' were heard but no one really spoke.

The servant, after closing all the doors and windows, returned to the doors from where he came in.

"Thank you Rolando," Fidel said as the servant closed the door behind him. "I want to make sure we are not disturbed."

"Great," Gutierrez whispered to Marcano. "This will be an all-nighter."

As if responding to his comment Fidel began. "I will be brief, at least with most of you. However with others…" His eyes were fixed on Marcano. "Let's just say that they will stay a little longer."

The comment received a few mumbles from the audience. Gutierrez nudge Marcano, making him blush.

The doors burst open and twenty soldiers rushed in; rifles ready. As the soldiers positioned themselves behind each member sitting around the table, a man walked in and closed the doors.

"Good evening, Colonel Guerra." Fidel Castro rose and walked to meet the man.

General Alarcon stood up to protest but was easily pushed back down to his chair by one of the soldiers.

Fidel nodded slightly and the soldiers placed their rifles on the floor. "Gentlemen," he said with a soft voice. "There's no reason to be alarmed. I simply want a military presence to witness this event." His smile began to put everyone at ease. He continued walking around the room, touching some of the guests as he walked behind them. "It seems that lately everyone is becoming a little restless about my health. The exile wants me dead and, I dare say some of you in this room as well."

The room remained silent.

"My concern is about the health of the revolution, and that…" He pointed a finger up as each soldier drew their side arm and fired directly on the head of the man sitting in front of them.

"Jesus!" Marcano shouted as a cloud of gunpowder filled the room.

The soldiers put their side arms back in their holsters and picked their rifles back from the floor.

After a nod from Fidel, Guerra barked an order and the soldiers quickly left the room.

Raul now walked near Marcano. "What's wrong Jose? Is this too uncivilized for you?"

"No, I mean…"

"Save it!" Raul shouted walking away and standing next to the man in the expensive suit.

Fidel, after walking around the table sat back on his chair. "Ever since I was fighting in *Sierra Maestra* I knew that I was…" Castro stopped himself noticing Marcano's tears.

"Oh, I guess you wouldn't understand; would you?" He shook his head slightly. "Of course you wouldn't. You think you're too important, making your deals with the Spanish, Canadians, and even the American."

"Fidel, I never—"

"Oh, please. Do you think you are the first that's ever gone this far? Do you think you are so special, with your deals and treachery?" Castro shook his head slightly. "You see; you never struggled like I have. You never had to fight and struggle for the Revolution. You never had to hide while soldiers hunted you down like wild animals. You never saw your comrades, your brothers, dying around you; fighting for a cause they believe so strongly in, as I did. As I still do. You never struggled like we did so long ago."

Marcano was now sobbing.

"Let me explain something to you. I am Cuba, I am the Revolution." Castro pulled his sidearm and shot him on the forehead. "The revolution will live and die with me."

Colonel Guerra approached the two brothers. "It is done Comandante. Now what?"

"Now, General Guerra," Fidel said making a point at the new rank he had given to the man. "Now we prepare to make our oppressors pay."

Chapter 6

==================

"Steven, come in, come in." Jerry Henderson seemed upbeat yet he looked extremely tire. "Sorry, we're running a little late. Ever since the death of Gonzalez there's been a lot of activity."

Conner nodded as Henderson pointed for him to sit.

"Acosta won't be joining us. They have him answering some questions upstairs. You know how that is."

"Yeah," Conner answered. He was glad Acosta was being questioned. After his conversation with Ann Becker earlier this morning she asked him to get as much help from the FBI as possible. This meant that he would have to provide them with some information. Unfortunately Conner was not too sure whom to trust, besides Henderson.

"Well, look what the cat dragged in," a female voice said behind him.

Conner turned and immediately smiled. "Kim?"

"You guys know each other?" Henderson asked.

"Oh yeah!" Special Agent Kim Murray said smiling as she reached and hugged Conner.

"What happened to your hair?" Conner asked. "It was almost down to your waist the last time I saw you."

"It was getting in my way when I was kicking your butt."

Conner laughed noticing Henderson's look. "We were on different sides of an investigation back in…" Conner thought for a moment. "How long ago?"

"Too long," Murray interrupted.

Conner smiled, still staring at her. Except for the short, blonde hair, Murray looked exactly the same. Her big blue eyes, and silly looking smile made her look vulnerable, something she always used as an advantage.

"So you are the man they sent?" Her tone was truly sarcastic.

Conner smiled back at her.

"Anyway," Henderson interrupted. "Murray had made multiple contacts with different militant exile groups. For some reason they respect her, mostly because they think she's a loose cannon. Some of the leaders trust her and think of her as a friend in the FBI."

"You know me and Latin men," Murray winked.

Conner made a mental note to check Murray's records. Unless something drastic happened to her in the past few years, Murray would be a person he could trust. She would die before betraying her country.

A knock on the door made them all turn to notice Ricardo Aguila standing by the door.

"Hello," he said sheepishly.

Henderson introduced him to Conner, who immediately shook hands. The young Cuban man seemed a little shy at first.

"Aguila is our Cuban expert. He could tell you anything on current events, as well as Cuban history."

"That would be really helpful," Conner said.

"Since Acosta won't be joining us any time soon, we might as well get started." Henderson pulled a chair from the office next door and closed the door as he entered.

"Mr. Conner is here to ask for our help." Henderson began. "It seems that for the past few days our friends up in Langley have been having difficulty communicating with contacts in Cuba. Our current investigation seemed to parallel his, so we have been asked to give Mr. Conner our full support."

"Just like I've been given the same directive," Conner added.

"First order of business is Gonzalez. As you all know, Gonzalez was murdered yesterday during a meeting with our mystery man." Henderson pulled a picture from his desk and threw it on his desk. "We have no idea who this man is, except for the name of Ignacio, which Gonzalez mentioned when the man arrived. We found no prints in the apartment, except for Gonzalez's. DNA results will take a few more days.

"Is there any possibility I can get a copy of that picture?" Conner asked. "Maybe our people—"

"Already on it, we sent the picture to a few agencies. So far, nothing." Henderson continued standing, pacing slowly around the room. "Kim, before we get to you, we need to address something else."

Murray agreed; a tiny smile was noticeable when she looked at Conner.

"Conner, do you want to brief us on our two guests?" Henderson said, finally sitting down.

Conner seemed comfortable in his chair and made no attempt to get up. "Yesterday afternoon I visited the Coast Guard Base in Miami Beach. Apparently, the Cutter Manitou intercepted a raft with two Cuban migrants onboard. Preliminary report stated that both were dead by the time the cutter reached them. A man, holding a knife had a single gunshot wound to the head and a woman with multiple stab wounds. The Coast Guard could not find the gun."

Murray raised her hand; the smile again on her lips seemed a little mischievous.

"Yes, Ms. Murray," Conner said.

"And what interest does the CIA have on two Cuban migrants dead at sea?"

Conner smiled back, his blue eyes piercing intensely into hers. "According to an Ensign aboard Manitou, the woman was still alive. He reported that the woman asked for someone in the CIA and that she had valuable information for us."

"And?" she asked almost interrupting.

"She died before she was brought onboard. She never said anything else."

"Was she one of yours?" she continued her questioning.

"No she wasn't."

"There was something else. She mentioned a date, June 5th, 1958." Conner turned to Aguila. "Any idea?"

Aguila fixed his glasses before he spoke. "Well, there's nothing I can think of, but I could search for you."

"That would be great." Conner turned back to Henderson. "That's all I have so far."

Henderson stood up once again. "Okay, well according to our prelim report, she was responsible for that shot. There were traces of gunpowder on her fingers which leads us to believe that she shot him."

The sound of his cell phone startled Conner. Under other circumstances he would mute the phone and continue the meeting, but this ring was different, this ring was important.

"Sorry!" he said moving to a corner of the room. As he reached for the phone, Conner heard two other cell phones come to live as well.

"That's strange," Henderson said reaching for his phone.

Conner's phone went silent as a text appeared on the screen.

Trouble!!!
Call back immediately
A.B.

Conner cleared the message on the phone and was ready to call back when the door of the conference room burst opened.

"Something's happening in Cuba; it's all over the news!"

The reaction was immediate. Henderson picked up a remote from his drawer and pressed the 'power' button. Behind him, a small television came to life.

Conner dialed the number and turned to watch.

We are working feverishly to get someone on the island but currently all communications seem to be down.

To recap, there are unconfirmed reports of multiple explosions in the Presidential Palace in Havana. We do not know if anyone was inside however there are rumors, and we want to reiterate, rumors, that top Cuban leaders were conducting a meeting when the explosions occurred.

Again these are unconfirmed reports.

The reporter continued but Conner turned his attention to the conversation on the phone.

"Yeah, I just heard," he said glancing over at the group; now quiet watching the news reports. There was no video feed, no phone call from the island; the news anchor continued to repeat the information as a black and white picture of a building was inserted on the left side of the screen.

"Well, it's more serious than that but I'll explain in a few hours when I see you." Becker said.

Conner was ready to ask but his attention turned immediately to the room.

"Happy Veinte de Mayo," Aguila muttered.

Conner looked at the man, the phone no longer important. "What did you say?"

"Veinte de Mayo, it's—"

"Cuba's Independence Day!" Conner finished.

Chapter 7

=================

The local Miami stations preempted all programming to continue the coverage in Cuba. The video feed was of crowds in Miami, out in the streets celebrating and dancing as the reporter continued to repeat the same information.

The reports now confirmed that high officials in the Cuban government were in a closed-door meeting when the explosion occurred. It was also confirmed that many, if not all, were dead. Whereabouts of Fidel Castro remained unknown.

Jerry Henderson parked the black Chevrolet Suburban in the Ft. Lauderdale Executive Airport's hangar and shut the engine off. Conner, sitting on the passenger side remained quiet and pensive.

"So, do you want to tell me now what's bothering you?"

"Why do they still call it Little Havana?"

"Huh?" Conner's question took Henderson by surprise.

"I lived in Miami for years and now, as I drove by 'Calle Ocho,' right in the middle of 'Little Havana,'" I did not see a single Cuban shop. I saw signs for Nicaraguan restaurants, Peruvian stores, Colombian shops, but I barely saw any Cuban stores."

Henderson remained confused; his eyes were fixed on Conner, his face serious. Suddenly, he realized it. Conner was doing anything to avoid the problem.

"Steven, I can't help you out if you don't tell me what's really going on in the island. I know there's got to be more than what you're telling me."

Conner did not turn. "Sorry Jerry, I can't."

"Whatever happened to agencies working together? Homeland Security and all that stuff?"

"Jerry, I don't have anything for you. Right now it's all bits and pieces; we need something concrete before we bring it to you guys."

"What about the dead girl?"

Conner turned and faced him. "I don't know who she was."

Henderson believed him. "Throw me a bone, anything!"

"I do have a serious concern. Something that might give us problems in the near future, unless you do something about it." Conner's tone sounded angry. "How much do you trust your team?"

"Huh?" Henderson's voice sounded hurt. "Those three are the best I've ever worked with, they're good."

His words seem to have no effect.

"I trust them with my life."

"And the people working under them?"

"Look Steven, they are all good agents. I can vouch for them."

"Do me a favor Jerry; have each one checked out again."

Henderson opened his mouth in protest but Conner gave him no chance to speak.

"I know they are your people, and I know that you trust them but right now I need more than your trust. We're dealing with something too big for us to overlook anything. If you seriously want us to consider you part of the team in the future; we need to be certain on whom to trust."

"Or who to use?"

"If it comes down to that, yes!"

Henderson was silent.

"You know perfectly well that someone dropped the ball in the Gonzalez incident. True, maybe it was an honest mistake, maybe the killer was better than your people anticipated, or maybe…" He let the words die out, let Henderson have his own doubts.

"I see your point," Henderson finally answered.

"All I'm saying is that you need to check out your people again. Anyone you might have doubts on should be moved to another task. Let Murray take care of all the exile groups, but warn her to be cautious on the people around her. I trust Murray; I've worked with her in the past, and Aguila seemed honest enough. All I'm asking is for you to have anyone under them checked thoroughly."

"Agreed," Henderson said as the engines of an executive jet ended the conversation abruptly.

The plane stopped a few feet from the hangar as crew began immediately to move around it, getting it ready for immediate departure.

"I guess, I'll be seeing you in a few days," Conner said.

"What do we do with your car?" Henderson asked.

"Leave it in the building. It would be madness driving down to Miami to drop it off."

The doors to the planes open and a woman began to descend from the plane.

"Whoa, who is that?"

Conner turned around and noticed Becker walking towards them. "That, is someone you don't want to cross."

Henderson's mouth was slightly opened and Conner realized that the man was not listening to him.

Becker turned to face the wind as she brushed her short red hair away from her face. She was dressed in a casual blouse and a pair of cargo shorts; making her look more like a tourist than a professional. As she got closer, Conner could see the smile on her face.

"Mr. Henderson? Hi, Ann Becker," she said extending her hand.

"Welcome to Miami," Henderson said shaking it.

Conner remained silent, he was enjoying seeing Ann Becker in action; the happy, aloof young woman who was shaking hands with Henderson was only a role; one she played perfectly.

"Steven," she said kissing him on the cheek.

Conner's smile grew larger as he noticed the spark in her green eyes. *This is going to be interesting,* he thought.

"Wow, Miami. I can't wait to hit the beaches."

Conner noticed the look in Henderson's face and he decided to join Becker in her little game.

"Did you bring your bathing suit?"

"Of course, kind of small though. I have it in my pocket." She did not have to turn to know Henderson's reaction; she's seen it enough times.

Two men brought a couple of suitcase and handed them to Henderson, who immediately placed them in the Suburban.

"Ready when you are," Becker said reaching for the back door of the SUV.

"I thought?" Conner began to ask but Becker was already closing the door from the inside.

Henderson looked at Conner who seemed as confused as he was. The men boarded the SUV and closed their door.

"Plane's leaving. I'm staying," Becker said still sporting the smile.

Henderson watched her through the rearview mirror, as Becker got comfortable in the back seat.

As the engine of the Suburban came to life, Becker's tone changed. "Anything new?"

Conner shook his head, as he began to open the envelope Becker handed him.

"One of our birds took that about a few hours ago. The explosion destroyed most of the building."

Conner observed the picture carefully. "Too well planned, too much explosives…it's just too perfect." He placed the pictures back in the envelope and turned. "Has to be military."

"Precisely," Becker said. "I'm sure whoever is responsible will point the finger at us."

"Any ideas yet?"

"No, they are keeping very quiet."

Henderson continued to drive, listening to the conversation without giving any input.

"We've tried to get help from the outside, anyone with any type of connection in Cuba. Unfortunately, everyone is running scared." Becker took the envelope back from Conner. "The Spanish and Canadians could not confirm or deny any of the information we gathered. They seemed scared."

"Not to mention all the interest those countries have on the island."

Becker nodded. "We're not the only ones who lost contacts. We have information that MI-6, also lost people."

Conner's body was turned enough to see Becker. "What is it?"

"We were desperate. We lost two more."

"What? Who?"

"Jurado and Bustamante, we found a way to get them to the island. Jurado went in through one of our contraband connection while Bustamante flew in from Mexico. They were supposed to make contact within three hours of their arrival." Her voice became softer, even graver. "They never reported in."

Becker turned her eyes to the mirror, noticing Henderson quickly glance away. "Mr. Henderson, whatever you are investigating seems to be the only lead we have left."

Chapter 8

========================

"I love the view!" Becker said looking at the bay from Conner's hotel room window.

Conner smiled hanging up the phone. "They say thirty minutes," he informed her throwing the room service menu back on the table.

Henderson drove them back to Conner's car, where they immediately said good-bye and drove away. The FBI man knew that Becker was here to discuss other issues, things that they did not feel comfortable to include him in; at least not yet.

Conner did not check out of his room, nor did he return the car. He was expecting to be back in Miami by late afternoon or the following day since the FBI investigation was the only lead they had. In return, he was surprise to see Becker arriving instead.

Becker remained by the bay window, watching the ocean.

Conner stood by her, also watching the view. "How bad is it?"

Becker turned, her mind returning to their original conversation. "It's worst than I said before. MI-6 claims that one of their agents was shot, no questions asked. Whatever it is, it's really bad."

Conner remained silent, listening.

"Van Buren gave the go-ahead on Minerva."

Conner turned immediately. "Minerva? That program is so outdated that it will only—"

"Not the new one. We're masking it as a virus so it will be hard to detect. It will still follow the same protocols as the original so there is no chance of confusion."

"But how do we know who to send it to, or where?"

"Virus, silly." Becker punched Conner on the arm. "We're not only flooding the island but we're letting a strand go wild here in the US."

Conner thought for a second. The idea was crazy enough to work; yet he was still worried. Someone in the island knew enough to cause all these problems, someone that could possibly reply to this message. He decided not to bring it up. "So what else do you have?"

"Well, some of these might be pure coincidence," she said taking a small pack from her bag. "Others might be...well, grasping at straws."

"Oh, I'm supposed to say that some of the dates are pure assumptions. There were no correlations between important dates in Cuban history and current events. This might only show that there might be some hidden agenda known only to those making the decisions—"

"Let me guess, Ogden?"

Becker could not help but laugh. "Anyway, there were a few things that he found almost immediately."

"Such as?" he asked sitting on the table opening the folder.

"As you know, May 20th, Cuban Independence Day. Also the day of the big explosion in Havana."

Conner nodded.

"May 19, Jose Marti's birthday, and four different Cuban Nationals that died mysteriously in this country."

"Gonzalez?" Conner asked.

"Precisely."

"But what about that other guy, Alvarez?"

"Don't know. I told you this was all we've got in such short notice." Becker looked back down at the paper. "April 17, Bay of Pig Invasion and also." She removed a copy of a newspaper article titled, 'Explosion Destroys house of Music Diva.'

Becker began to read a caption. "At the time, Ms. Estevez was running errands with her daughter but the blast killed two people in the house. "

"Helena Estevez, yes I read the article, although it wasn't in the front page like it was here," Conner said standing and reaching for another paper on the table.

"Of course not. Here she is an icon, Cuban girl becomes star, what else can you ask for."

"Wasn't the explosion caused by a gas leak?"

"Yes, that was the report but check this out." She picked up the paper from the table and began to read. Ms. Estevez is a known anti-Castro advocate to the point that her music is not allowed in Cuba. Also, her father was one of the invaders during Bay of Pig."

Conner mouth was now open.

"Should I go on?"

He nodded, forcing his mouth closed.

March 13, a student protest ends in a massacre by Batista's men. March 13, Congresswoman Edith Rosenstein is killed in a car accident. Ms. Rosenstein was spearheading a new bill to make the embargo even tougher."

"Hold on," Conner said. It says here that it was a random DUI accident and the driver was killed—"

"There were 4 full gas canisters in the trunk of the car."

"How far did you check?" Conner asked.

"Couple more." She looked at the paper again. "Let me see, March 10, Batista takes over. March 10, a live grenade explodes during an exercise in an anti-Castro paramilitary training. Seven people died, including one of our guys." She saw a few more, skipping them. "Here's another one. February 24, Radio Rebelde; goes on the air. That's the Rebel radio station that Castro started during his days fighting Batista's men in Sierra Maestra."

"Wasn't that the date of the Radio Marti incident?" Conner asked.

"Yup."

"I think we have some kind of pattern."

"This one is a gem. Remember the incident in DC? Somehow, someone managed to throw a can of yellow paint into Lincoln's statue."

"Yes, there were blaming some new gang that was leaving graffiti almost everywhere."

"Well," Becker tossed the paper onto Conner's lap. "Check this one out."

"US Marine climbs on a statue of Jose Marti and urinates on it?" Conner was stunned. "What the–"

Becker did not let him finish. "The outrage was immediate, and protestors took to the streets, including a young law student name Fidel Castro." She eyed the paper again. "I could go on."

"What about June 5, 1958?" Conner asked.

"Oh yes, the letter." Becker handed Conner a copy of a letter. "Ogden found this letter written by Castro himself."

Conner noticed the length of the letter and put it aside. "We'll get to that later. What else do we have?"

"June 14th, Che Guevara's birthday; July 12th, The Manifesto of Sierra Maestra. Of course, like I said; this could be important dates or it could be nothing. It all depends on who is responsible."

"I think we know who is responsible. The question is; what is he planning."

"Or why?"

"Whatever it is, we don't have much time. If this pattern continues, we only have until July 26th."

Becker nodded. "The most important date in Castro's Cuba' the movement, the revolution, everything to them."

"It's what started it all; the attack on the Moncada Barracks." Conner moved to the window, his eyes looking into the horizon. "A small group or rebels attacked a target that they had no chance of defeating. Men willing to die for their cause." Conner turned back to Becker. "I think we might have a huge problem."

Becker's eyes had the same worried look as Conner's.

"What if July 26th is the culmination? What if the US Naval Base at Guantanamo is the new Moncada?"

Chapter 9

================

A ray of sunshine danced on Conner's face as the curtain moved in unison with the air conditioning. He let his eyes get adjusted to the light, his mind slowly returning to the night before. There was not much to think as he noticed Becker's body lying next to him.

So much for the breakup, he thought kissing her on the back of the neck.

Her body moved slightly but she continued sleeping.

Conner moved away from the bed and picked up his cell phone, which he left charging on the dresser. Noticing that he had two text messages waiting, he entered a password and began to read.

Minerva to go live at 6:00 AM EST

He deleted the message and selected the next one.

Minerva alert!

Whether the message would give them hope or bring more headaches remained to be seen. At this time, all they could do was wait.

Conner sat on the chair, and picked up the letter. He planned to read it the night before but after dinner things slowly turned his attention to a more important matter, now lying in the bed sleeping.

He read each sentence slowly, checking and double checking for any hidden meaning but finding none. The phone, sitting on the adjoining table, began to vibrate and he picked it up immediately. Conner read the message and immediately saved it.

"Hey," the raspy voice called from the bed.

"Good morning sleepy head," Conner said putting the phone and letter back on the table.

"Who was that?"

He moved to the bed and sat next to her. "Seems like we're having a conference call at 3:00 PM today, which gives you some time to enjoy the beach."

"Good," she said closing her eyes once again.

He smiled watching her stretch. "Rough night?"

"Nothing I couldn't handle," she replied dragging him towards her.

Juan Navarro sat starring at the monitor screen as he waited for the system to process his entry. The computer took between 30 seconds to almost 2 minutes to process the information that took him little over 10 seconds to input. It was a long wait, but one that Navarro cherished allowing his mind to wander off. Of course he often wondered if it wouldn't be easier for him to use a typewriter and file the information himself. He shouldn't complain, in contrast, some of his coworkers were still using more antiquated CRT's.

"Ay coño!" a voice yelled from somewhere within the maze of cubicles, followed by another.

"We have a virus!" someone else said.

Navarro opened his e-mail program and noticed the suspicious e-mail. Curiously, he read the subject field of the message wondering if he would've noticed that this was a virus. As different people continued to curse after opening the attachment promising nude pictures, the message caused a different reaction in Navarro.

Removing a diskette from his drawer, Navarro placed it in the computer and returned to the message. As the mouse hovered over the attached file, Navarro typed a string of keys and watched as a message appeared: SAVING.

Another person cursed as Navarro's hand quickly typed a second string of character not unlike the ones used in his system.

Navarro used this program before, why it was delivered in the form of a virus was strange, but not a total surprise. Quietly, he had been waiting for some type of communication, and this was definitely it.

A small box appeared and Navarro typed a codename quickly. He pressed the button again and the virus disappeared from his screen as the diskette continued to spin.

"I have the virus too," he shouted removing the diskette from his computer and placing it in his pocket. "What do I do?"

"Don't touch it!" A man said hurrying to his location.

As the virus continue to find more computers to infect, a small electronic signal found its way out of the Cuban electric company's network and began a return trip back to its originator. The network became overwhelmed and a few minutes later the entire electric company's network came crashing down.

"Watch it!" Conner shouted as Becker shifted the car to a lower gear and cut across two lanes. Shifting again, she accelerated and left the slower cars behind.

"I love this car," she shouted back at Conner. "I love the rush of the wind in my hair, and this weather."

Conner did not respond, watching the road as Becker continued to push the fast sports car to its limit.

"So how close are we going to be to the Air Force Base?" Becker asked.

"It's an Air Reserve now, and according to the GPS it will be only a few miles." Conner felt his stomach settling as he began to get used to Becker's driving. It wasn't the first time he sat on the passenger seat with Becker at the wheel. It was however the first time she'd driven this way.

The early afternoon traffic was lighter now that the car was distancing itself from the actual city. In the distance, a crew of workers was changing a billboard, announcing a weekend block party. The colorful sign announced a party to celebrate the new dawn in Cuban history. The festivities in Miami had continued since the news from Cuba was broadcasted. After two days of chaos, the city decided to find some way of returning the citizens to some sense of calm by throwing another "Calle 8" style party. Using the same location as the 8th Street Block Party, the celebration would culminate all the festivities that have sprung around the city.

Conner shook his head.

"What?" Becker asked.

"I just think that this city is in for a big disappointment."

"Why?" She asked quizzically. "Even after the president sent his condolences, there was no response from the island. So who knows what's really happening."

"It's too quiet. Nobody has come forward, not even the military. All I know is that whenever he shows up, this city will not be happy."

"Why do you say that, he might be dead you know."

Conner shook his head again. "No, I think he is having his fun. But I think that this celebration might be exactly what he is looking forward. Bet you anything Castro will surface before this celebration starts."

"Why?"

"Because, what better way to destroy these people's hope?" He glanced at the GPS and back at the road. "Turn here."

The car turned up a dirt road leading to a large house. As they moved closer Conner noticed the open field around the house.

"Definitely farm country," Becker said.

The car came to rest next to a large semi, parked on the side of the house. As Becker opened the door of the car, a tall, large, blonde man opened the front door. Conner recognized the man as Harry Hawkins, an ex-Army Ranger who Van Buren recruited over a year ago. He was dressed casually, but even now Hawkins continued to act like a soldier.

The man led the guests into the house where they were given a small tour. Conner's bedroom was next to Becker's while the other three bedrooms were on the opposite end of the house.

"How convenient," Becker whispered with a devilish smile.

"Anything on Minerva?" Conner asked smiling back at Becker.

"System will be up in another 10-15 minutes. We should have an answer by then."

As suspected, Minerva made its way to Cuba and the virus was causing havoc on the island. A second strand of the virus hit the US an hour before. The 'Symantec' website's Virus Metrics assessed the virus as a High Distribution but Low Damage threat. The last report confirmed that Minerva was more of an annoyance than a security risk.

The agent led them through the back sliding door and around a large swimming pool. As they walked to a small guesthouse the engine of the trailer came to life. "I guess they're done," he said as the trailer began to move away.

"Where's everyone else?" Becker asked.

"Dexter is setting up all his hardware," Hawkins said. "You know him and computers."

The two agents nodded.

"Tamargo went to the stores to buy some groceries. Something about that guy and cooking."

Conner did not know who the man was and made a mental note to check him out later. "Where's Van Buren?"

"Oh yes!" Hawkins said smiling as he took an envelope from his pocket.

Conner opened the envelope and removed the card. The words caught him by surprise.

You're in charge!

"Congrats!" Becker said smiling.

Conner turned to face her. "You knew?"

The exchange lasted only a few seconds as the door of the guesthouse burst open and Dexter came out.

Conner began to say hello, but Dexter grabbed him and rushed him in.

"Van Buren wants to talk to you, now."

Chapter 10

====================

C onner was expecting a few computers around the room but was completely shocked when he walked into the room.

A small conference table sat in the middle of the room, which seemed bare but for the large plasma screen monitor facing the head of the conference table. Conner looked around but saw no other equipment.

"Everything is in the room next door," Dexter explained. "I figure we can have our meetings here while everything is hidden next door."

Conner nodded, realizing that the picture on the large screen was that of Van Buren.

"Good afternoon, sir." Conner sat on the head of the table.

Van Buren was dressed in his dark grey business suit, something he always did when he was conducting important meetings. His white beard was nicely trimmed, which along with his wavy white hair made him look less like a businessman and more like a mythological god. His face alone made him look like an imposing figure. Those who weren't intimidated by his look were soon frightened by his booming voice.

"Conner," Van Buren replied. "I want us to talk before this meeting starts."

"Yes sir, and thank you."

Van Buren said nothing, his eyes staring at Dexter.

"Ah, I just remember that I have to finish something," Dexter said walking out of the guesthouse.

Van Buren waited until Dexter closed the door before he continued. "We have a full house so I need you to be ready. Both, the Chairman of the Joint Chiefs and the National Security Advisor, have some questions for you. I know both the Secretary of Defense and Secretary of State will be there as well; maybe even the president."

Conner felt Van Buren's piercing eyes beginning to sting him.

"I need you to remain calm during this meeting. This people are going to say a lot of garbage, things that will irritate everyone but you can't let them get to you. They are politicians above all."

"Yes, sir."

"But if you decide to explode, make sure you have the evidence to back it up."

"Yes, sir."

"So what exactly do you have?"

"As you know the cigar tube was definitely one of ours. Whoever sent it, knew exactly how to handle it."

Van Buren remained silent.

I believe that the message was written in that fashion only to remind whoever was carrying it on what to say. Maybe even an important detail. I don't think that it was what they hoped to deliver."

"Go on," Van Buren's voice boomed through the speakers.

"I think Castro is alive and he will resurface soon."

"What makes you say that?" Van Buren asked.

"First: the dates in the message. All dates are relevant to the Cuban Revolution, something that would be important to him but not to one of the, so called, 'new bloods.' Second: most of the Cuban nationals killed in the past few days were Marcano sympathizers. As you know Marcano was slowly gaining a lot of popularity in the island. Third: the reference to the letter. I found a caption in a letter from Fidel Castro to Celia Sanchez, it says: 'I've sworn that the Americans are going to pay dearly for what they are doing. When this war is over a much wider and bigger war will begin for me, the war I am going to wage against them.' It sounds like a declaration of war."

"That was written a long time ago. He is talking about the revolution."

Conner put the paper down. "It is the promise he never kept, a promise to friends now long gone."

"Continue."

"Sir, my best estimate is that, if Castro does resurface, he might have a hidden agenda, something that he might have planned a long time ago. Guantanamo has always been a thorn on his side; after all he hasn't cashed any of the checks he's received as payment for the land. I think that attacking and taking over Gitmo would be something he would love to see, before he dies."

"If this is the case, we need to be very careful when we bring this up in the meeting."

"Sir, there's something else."

Van Buren said nothing, watching Conner, as he remained silent.

"If Castro is so bold as to attack an American military installation, then why would he stop there? The Cubans in Miami are as much an annoyance as that base is."

"Conner," Van Buren thundered. "Castro could be many things, but one thing he is not is an idiot. Attacking a military base will have great repercussions, and attacking Miami—"

"But think about it sir. If he attacks and takes over Gitmo, even for an hour, he will have a 'unified Cuba,' his lifelong dream. If he attacks Miami, he will be the first foreign country ever to succeed in a military attack against the continental US." Conner paused slightly waiting for some kind of response.

He got none. "This will not be some kind of terrorist attack, but a full military attack, an act of war from one nation to another. Think of it as another Pearl Harbor."

"Alright, here's one question for you. Why?"

"Marcano. It all goes back to Marcano. The man became too popular, too fast. Castro saw him as a real threat. He also knows that he is too old to continue fighting these types of battles. Castro was a fighter and although he has been in power for so long, the fighting is still in him. After all, what better way to finish than this way?"

"July 26, the beginning and the end of Castro's Revolution." Van Buren said matter-of-fact.

"All Cubans, no matter where they live, will remember this date in happiness and sadness."

The house was deserted, as it was every day when Juan Navarro arrived from work. He remembered weeks ago, when even dying of old age; his old dog would come and greet him by the door. Navarro missed him, being the only true friend and confidant.

The glow of the television illuminated the dark room as Navarro opened a half spent bottle of rum and walked to his bedroom.

Leaving the lights off, he moved to the corner of the room where an old computer sat in a beat up makeshift table. The computer, built from spare parts he acquired at work, was more than enough for him. He was one of the privileged ones, as he could think of only two other people with a computer at home.

There was no Internet connection, no access to his office from the system; in fact all he had was a small word processing system and a few solitaire games. The computer, in fact, was more for show than for use.

The warm, green glow of the monitor began to flood the bedroom. He made certain that all the windows were closed before he proceeded to push the mattress off the bed.

Placing two small rods between the borders of a slightly loose tile, he lifted it up to reveal a compact disc inside a small plastic bag.

The procedure was simple and Navarro had performed it a few times in the past, but not in nearly a year. He knew that they would contact him; so much has happened in the past few days that he knew it was inevitable.

He inserted the disc in the computer and waited for the program to start. A list of folders appeared on the screen and Navarro selected the one he was searching for: 'cutieluv.' The name was the same found on the Subject Field of the e-mail received earlier, a name that immediately alerted Navarro.

He placed the diskette inside the computer and clicked on the virus. The diskette began to spin.

"You have been hit by the Minerva virus!!!!!"

Navarro held the Ctrl and Alt keys simultaneously as he typed his personal code. The message was immediately replaced by another one.

"Urgent!!!

All communication lost...need assistance.

Follow protocol V61."

Navarro pressed a button and the message disappeared.

He formatted the diskette and after removing it from the computer he let it shatter in his hand. The plastic would be thrown away; the actual disc would burn along with dinner.

Protocol V61 was simple, "trust no one, gather information, and await contact." Navarro had seen this message before during the Cold War, but that was so long ago.

Once everything was hidden Navarro began to prepare his dinner. He knew that the situation was critical; he also knew that due to the lack of information in the message; nobody was being trusted.

He wished there was a way he could send a message back, not as a signal but telling them he could be trusted.

His file was probably being read at this very moment, a stranger going through his entire life, studying all his record. By now someone had made a decision on him. He wondered if he would hear from them again.

Marcie! His mind finally screamed.

Since the virus arrived Navarro had been thinking about himself, first worried on being caught, then worried about not being trusted. Now, he realized something his mind had tried to ignore for days.

The message was urgent, and due to the lack of actual information Navarro realized that Marcie never made it to the States.

Chapter 11

=================

Steven Conner felt the eyes of his team watching him, waiting for some kind of answer.

He returned from the meeting quiet, devastated, his mind going over everything that was said, again and again.

It was easy to see, the look in Van Buren's eyes was enough to tell him that the meeting was going extremely well. Everyone present remained silent as he detailed what he believed would be the next step. Everything was going extremely smooth, until.

The Secretary of Defense however had a different agenda. Within seconds of Conner's conclusion, the old, almost senile man, began a campaign to destroy every single point Conner had mentioned minutes before.

At first, Conner saw an allied in the Chairman of the Joint Chiefs; but the man soon became silent, and his voice was not heard from again. Conner's temper was slowly rising and he tried to relax, ignoring some of the insults the old man was viciously firing back at him. He was keeping his cool, trying desperately to keep from returning the insults. The effort was heroic, but at the end, it was unsuccessful.

"Listen, you pompous ass." Conner noticed Van Buren's face moved slightly downward as his eyes were no longer looking at the camera. On the other monitor, the Secretary of Defense tried to hide a smile. "Everything I've said has been researched and verified. There are people out there, whose lives have either ended, or are in serious danger. Something is happening on that island, something that will threaten the safety of this country. You however, are so damn nearsighted that you can't see danger if it's standing in front of you."

Conner was no longer looking at any of the other monitors. His rage was only directed at one monitor, the one with a completely shocked Secretary of Defense. "The fact is that, the danger exists, not thousands of miles away but here, in our own backyard. The danger is not from some terrorist driving a truck or a plane into a building, but rather that of a full military attack against us. This is not some derange madman trying to follow some divine plan from Allah or some other god, but rather a very astute, calculating man who has given this country decades of headaches."

The old man began to protest but Conner stopped him almost immediately.

"We are here to find any threats against this country and to make each one of you aware. I know that something will happen. Castro will resurface, in less than five days, and when he does, he will have a well-planned agenda. These attacks will continue, and they will increase. If we don't act now, we will be unprepared later on.

"Mr. Conner!" the old man interrupted, his voice almost shouting. "Castro is dead, the island will be in chaos in a few days and when someone finally takes control we will take the appropriate actions." The old man's finger was resting on the button. "This concludes this meeting."

The monitor soon went dark, followed by another one.

Conner noticed that Van Buren was still there, and also the Chairman of the Joint Chiefs.

"Mr. Conner," the man's voice boomed. "If you are right, we will need some kind of a plan."

"I am aware of it sir, and I am right."

"If that's the case, we'll see you sometime next week." The Chairman smiled as his screen went blank.

Van Buren's monitor remained on, the man watching him closely. "Two things," he said raising two fingers. "One, you have to learn to play politics; however I don't think you made an enemy, but rather a friend."

Conner looked back at the screen quizzical.

"Two, keep working with the FBI and whatever you have on Minerva. That's all we have to work on, for now."

The screen went blank as well, leaving Conner alone with his thought.

= = = = =

As he returned to the main house, Conner was unusually quiet, something everyone dismissed as the responsibilities of the new job.

Everyone allowed him some space, leaving him alone and not talking. Even Becker who knew well enough it wasn't really the responsibilities bothering him.

Conner finally met Anthony Tamargo, a young Latin man who seemed more at home in the kitchen than discussing sensitive information. Son of a Cuban mother and Puerto Rican father, Tamargo seemed like a natural for this particular operation. As Tamargo ended his duties in the kitchen with a fresh pot of Cuban coffee, the team gathered around the table. Minerva had returned with only two contacts before it stopped transmitting. It was the best news Conner had all day.

Dexter returned with two files and all the information they had on the two men that responded.

The team agreed almost unanimously on Eduardo Peralta, a twenty-something year old young man who lost his parent when he was a teenager. Peralta made a name for himself by supplying information on weapons Cuba was purchasing from North Korea.

Although the information was not valuable, Peralta became an asset to them. In contrast, Juan Navarro was the complete opposite. Already in his mid-forties, Navarro had been one of the main contacts in the island for years. Most of the important information came either from him, or one of the assistants he recruited in the past. For some strange reason, a few years ago, Navarro's name slowly began to fade.

Conner was grateful on the teams' immediate decision. It was a good way of dismissing them, letting them think they had accomplished something.

Within minutes Hawkins and Tamargo left the house. It was early on a weekend night and both agents wanted a taste of South Beach. Dexter returned to his computers, the only love he had, the only thing he cared about.

"Hey," Becker whispered in his ear, her hands rubbing his shoulders.

Conner held her hand and squeezed it tight.

"What's troubling you?"

He remained quiet, his eyes fixed on the two files.

"Besides the meeting?" Becker added.

"I don't know," he said honestly. "Something here is bothering me; something I can't seem to find."

She went around and sat next to him. Taking one of the files she began to read.

"Hey guys," Dexter said walking past them. "Just getting some milk and cookies before bed."

The short, longhaired man walked around in a pair of blue pajamas making Becker turned away trying not to laugh.

Navarro took another sip of rum from the bottle to numb his palate. After turning the television set off he sat back on the chair; darkness creeping into the room as the light of the television began to fade. It was dark, not unlike that night.

He had arrived home around midnight after three hours of interrogation in the local militia station. The interrogation was done by Cuban Intelligence; it immediately raised Navarro's curiosity. He was worried when he was picked-up; thinking that all those years of spying for the Americans had finally caught up with him. Instead he was surprised at the reason for his arrest, his relationship with a woman named Maria Cecilia Fernandez.

He was released near midnight when the agents realized that he had no useful information; they were mistaken.

"I know you're here," he said walking into the darkness that was his house.

She said nothing, hugging him almost immediately.

"Why are they looking for you?" he asked her.

"It's not only me. They're picking everyone up."

Navarro frowned trying to figure out why they let him go.

"I shouldn't be here," she said finally.

"No! You're safe. They already paid me a visit."

"I know, I'm sorry," she said apologetically.

"Goes with the job."

"I need to contact the Americans. Something is happening."

Navarro pretended not to care, she knew better.

"I'm leaving, Juan," she said finally.

Again, he said nothing.

"One of my contacts has a way to get us out of the island. Once there I can make contact."

He was unmoved.

"Come with me," she said hugging him again.

"There's nothing for me there."

"There's nothing for you here."

His hands were around her, but not holding her.

"I'll be there." Fernandez pushed herself against him. "I need you, I've always had."

"No," he said finally. "You proved a long time ago that you could handle yourself well."

She smiled at him kissing him on the cheek.

"When are you leaving?" he asked.

"Soon, maybe tomorrow."

"Then," he said. "We need to get you ready."

He sat on the table and motion for her to sit next to him. "Tell me what you know."

"I have a contact," she began. "Colonel Rogelio Berrios. We met two days ago; he was very agitated. He told me that they were mobilizing units to Oriente."

"That's nothing new," Navarro interrupted.

"I said the same but he was worried. He told me that two of his commanders were removed and new ones were brought up."

"Again, nothing new."

Fernandez nodded. "The new commander is Colonel Fernando Chavez."

"Fernando Chavez?" Navarro asked alarmed. "I thought he had been discharged two years ago."

There was no reason for Navarro to ask the question, he was more than aware of the story behind Chavez. It had been Navarro who found Chavez' plot and warn the Americans, a move that almost cost him his life. He warned them again and again, but nobody seemed to listen, or to care, asking him instead more information on the Cuban-Colombian Drug Cartel connection.

After losing two of his friend and narrowing escaping a trap that Navarro knew only happened due to the misinformation from an American agent, he turned his attention back to Chavez. It was then that Navarro realized that Chavez had an agenda of his own, something that Navarro used against the Colonel. If the Americans were no longer listening, Navarro had to find other ways to stop this madman.

The Cuban government arrested Chavez and charged him with drug trafficking. Only a selected few knew the real reasons for his arrest. As Chavez was sentenced to life in prison, the American government tried to contact Navarro with an apology. He was no longer listening.

"Berrios told me that he has been put in charge of all mechanized divisions." Fernandez continued.

Navarro scribbled something on a paper and went back to his bedroom. He returned with a cigar box.

"What is that?" Fernandez asked.

Navarro ripped the paper and showed it to her.

Fechas Del pasado - AHORA
Importante – 5 de Junio 1958
Guantanamo

Fernandez frowned looking at the paper. "I understand the last line, but what do the other two mean?"

"I've been seeing a pattern, something subtle that is slowly becoming more obvious."

"You haven't lost your touch, have you?"

Navarro smiled. "When you make contact, tell them to check some of the dates, look for some kind of pattern."

Fernandez was still confused.

"Mention Batista's escape from Cuba, Batista taking over. Tell them to check those dates; the rest will fall into place." Navarro paused for a second looking into Fernandez' eyes. "If you tell them everything, they won't trust you. Make them do the research."

Fernandez nodded. "What about the date?"

"It's the closest thing to a declaration of war that has ever been said by Castro. Enough to make them get off their fat asses."

Fernandez smiled.

Navarro removed a tube from the box and unscrewed it. He placed the paper and closed it once again. "Here," he said handing it to Fernandez. "Keep it by your side, but don't let anyone else see it and whatever you do, don't open it."

"What is it?"

"It's your ticket to freedom. It should guarantee your stay and will make them believe you."

She looked at the tube slowly. "This is a fake," she said finally.

"Yes, it's also sealed. The only one that can open it is someone with the experience—"

"You mean—" she interrupted him, her eyes widening.

"CIA," he said.

She continued looking at the tube, her eyes inspecting every inch.

Navarro took another object from the box. "Here," he said handing her a small revolver. "You might need it."

Think! Conner's mind shouted.

Three hours had past and he was still sitting by the table, the two folders opened in front of him.

He shared a laugh with Becker, after Dexter left. An hour later he took her to her bedroom, avoiding her advances as his mind continued to go over the files. The meeting had been a disaster and Conner was determined not to screw this up too.

Conner picked a bottle of water from the refrigerator and twisted the cap. His hand was squeezing the bottle too hard and water spilled out around him. Closing the cap again, he reached for a paper towel. "That's it!" he almost shouted. "That's the missing piece."

Chapter 12

==================

The lights of the city were barely visible from the darkened Atlantic. A moonless night made the distant lights of Miami tiny specs as if stars were also shining on the horizon.

Below, where the lights would not dare penetrate, a dark silhouette moved swiftly as the propeller left behind a small wake. The nuclear-powered submarine, *San Juan*, hugged the coast of South Florida, waiting to move out to sea. Part of the USS Enterprise Strike Group, the *San Juan* purposely separated from the group as it prepared for the upcoming exercise.

"You sure about this skipper?" the XO asked sipping his coffee.

Raymond McNeil smiled as his officer continued to question him.

"So you intend to ride on the *Vicksburg's* wake as she leaves Port Everglade?"

"It's too simple. The cruiser has been having problem with their sonar since they arrived back from the Gulf. The problem will not be fixed until she returns to Groton but she will be part of the exercise." McNeil scratch the back of his neck, feeling a hint of sunburn. "The crew will still be talking about the whole 'Fleet Week' in Florida so they won't suspect a thing."

"I can't believe Masterson let you do this."

The conversation was cut short by the call.

"Conn, sonar." The sonar chief's voice sounded strange.

"What is it Williams?" McNeil asked.

The pause was more than evident. "Skipper, I think you should come and see this."

McNeil moved immediately causing his officer to almost drop his coffee.

"Skipper?" his officer asked.

"Williams shouldn't be on sonar, I told him to rest until the exercise. Something's up."

McNeil arrived immediately, noticing his sonar chief in front of the screen, a sonar man standing beside him.

"Report!" McNeil said as he arrived.

Williams looked at his sonar man; the young man began to speak. "Sir, I was tracking a contact heading out from Miami. I believe it was some kind of pleasure yacht or cruise." The boy looked uncomfortable but McNeil said nothing. "The ship was heading..." The sonar man fumbled through a paper but Williams took over.

"He noticed a new contact, and he called me immediately." The sonar chief pressed a button allowing the contact to be shown on the screen. "Anyway, I thought you should take a look."

"I'll be damn!" McNeil said frowning.

It wasn't hard for McNeil to see why Williams called him. On the screen, among dots and bars McNeil noticed what Williams was referring to. Impossible to see by most, to the trained eye, or the person that spent his career tracking this type of target it was obvious.

"It's a Russian sub, isn't it?" the young sonar man asked.

Williams patted the young man on the back. "Alpha Class," he said. "A really fast attack boat. Actually still holds the record in—"

"Williams!" McNeil interrupted. "You can give him the history lesson later; right now I want that Alpha tracked."

"Already on it, skipper." Williams said.

"Question is what is an Alpha doing this far from home?" McNeil said.

"I thought they were all retired," the XO almost interrupted.

"Apparently not," replied McNeil.

"Should we report this?" the executive officer asked.

McNeil did not wait for a response. "Hell no! First we find out what they're up to."

As the USS San Juan changed headings to follow the Alpha, on the surface, the passengers aboard the pleasure cruise *Infatuation* continued to enjoy their expensive dinner.

"Gentlemen, gentlemen. I'm sure we are all very eager to begin, but we need to follow the agenda as scheduled."

"But why do we need to wait until the end of dinner for the elections, let's do it now." a voice asked somewhere in the back.

"What's your hurry Garcia? It's not like Castro is going to come out of the grave."

Laughter erupted from the entire room as a short stocky man got up.

"Yes?" The man in the podium pointed at him. "How can we help you mister?"

"My name is George Suarez, I have a question."

"And you are here, how?"

"Oh, I'm sorry. I received an invitation for this cruise." Suarez seemed to be as confused as the man in the podium as for his reason of being here.

"Very well, I guess if you received an invitation you have as much right to be here as the rest of us." The man's voice said with a hint of sarcasm.

"Oh, okay." Suarez said. "I am trying to figure out what this is all about."

"I'm sorry; I don't seem to understand your question."

"Very well," Suarez replied, his voice sounding more confident now. "I see on this page that some of the bullets for this meeting deal with current events in Cuba. Although I don't see the relevance, I do understand that there might be a point to it." He walked closer to the podium, noticing that he had the full attention of the entire crowd.

"There are a few points that I need to understand."

"Such as?" the speaker asked.

"Well, like this one for instance," Suarez asked pointing at a section in the paper he was holding. "It says here, transitional government. What exactly are you referring to?"

"Exactly what it says there. We are voting tonight for President and Vice President of the new Cuban transitional government."

"Excuse me?"

"What part don't you understand?"

"You mean to tell me that we'll be voting for the future President and Vice-President of Cuba?"

"That's exactly what we'll be doing."

"And who gave you all the authority to represent the entire Cuban community?"

"We plan to submit our results to the US government; they will have the last saying."

"But what about the Cubans?"

"We'll bring this to the community, both in Miami and New Jersey. We'll also make this information available through the country for any Cuban leaving outside those areas. We don't foresee a problem since we represent a great majority."

Suarez looked around the room, "I'm sorry but I don't see anyone here that seems to represent me, but again that's not my question. You are forming a Cuban government right here, right now?"

"Yes, we feel that after Castro's death, we should make it our number one priority." The speaker was beginning to get annoyed.

"Get to the point!" a voice screamed.

"Don't you see it; you are all planning this government not even considering what the people in Cuba need."

"The Cubans in the US will know; the ones in Cuba…"

"Yes, what about the ones in Cuba?" Suarez asked.

"They don't know what they want; they don't understand what they need."

"And you do?" Suarez looked around the room trying to get some support but received none. "Seriously, you are planning to walk into a country in turmoil and claim to be the new president?"

"Sit down!" another voice yelled.

"That doesn't make you guys any different than Castro."

"What!" the speaker yelled.

"All these years you have been crying of how Cuba has no choices, no elections, no saying and you are planning to do the exact same thing."

"He's a communist!" a voice shouted in anger.

"Who the hell is this guy?" another one asked.

"Calm down, all of you!" the speaker announced. "Mr. Suarez, is it? The people of Cuba have been under the reign of this tyrant for too long. They don't know about freedom, nor do they know what a democratic election is. We are doing this to help them, to guide them in the right direction."

"You are doing this to exploit them, just like your predecessor." Suarez replied noticing two men approaching him. "All you want to do is get your companies inside before anyone else, get a monopoly started before the country even realizes it."

"That's enough!" the speaker shouted as the two men grabbed Suarez.

"Throw him overboard!" another voice said.

"Peter," the speaker shouted to one of the two men. "Find out who invited him here."

Chapter 13

=================

San Juan was keeping its distance from the Russian Alpha, as McNeil tried to avoid detection. He was an expert in this type of tactics, seeing himself in this type of situation countless of times. The current target, however, bothered him. Noisy and slow, the Alpha was running unlike any submarine he ever tracked. To McNeil, the skipper was either not concerned with being stealthy, or too concerned with whatever his mission was.

McNeil's worries soon became more evident.

"Torpedo in the water!" Williams shouted.

McNeil turned, not really surprised. "Range?"

Williams' hand was raised as if to interrupt the skipper. "Sir, the heading is, 178."

"Ron, get me a solution, I want two torpedoes in their tubes now."

"Sir, torpedoes have acquired a target."

"What?" McNeil turned back.

"They're going for that cruise ship."

"Must be some kind of accident," the XO suggested.

"There doesn't seem to be any change in direction."

"Another torpedo in the water!"

"Tubes ready sir."

"Ron, I need a solution," McNeil said annoyed.

"90 percent. That Alpha is just sitting there."

"FIRE!"

"Torpedoes away sir," the XO replied almost immediately.

Williams' eyes were fixed on the screen, his fingers dancing on the console. McNeil watched as the man seemed to become part of the console. "Sir, first detonation. Direct hit on the ship."

McNeil moved closer to his Sonar Chief.

"Our torpedoes have acquired." Williams said. "Alpha turning hard to port."

"There's got to be some kind of a mistake. Maybe he was trying to attack us." The Executive Officer continued to look for a reason to the attack.

"Second detonation. Two direct hits on cruise ship." Williams continued to describe the situation. "Alpha is deploying countermeasures."

McNeil knew that the Alpha countermeasures were probably outdated, making it impossible for the boat to slip away from *San Juan's* new MK type torpedoes.

"Torpedo one reacquiring." Not five seconds later, Williams spoke again. "Torpedo two reacquiring."

McNeil felt the anger rising as Williams announced the distance between the two MK torpedoes and the Alpha submarine. "Get me two more torpedoes; that bastard is not getting away."

"Direct hit sir." Williams paused, waiting for some kind of a signal. "Alpha destroyed sir."

There was no shout, no applause, and no celebration. The team was quiet and shocked, everyone remaining in the exact same position.

It was McNeil who spoke first. "Well done everyone."

There were a few nods of acknowledgement, everyone still quiet.

"Take us up, we need to find survivors and report this."

The sound of the telephone in the house and his cellular phone ringing simultaneously awoke Conner immediately. As he picked up his cell phone, he noticed Becker running into his bedroom alarmed.

The voice on the phone was direct and precise, waiting for no questions, or comments. Conner acknowledged and hung up the phone.

"What was that?"

"There's been an incident. Van Buren will be calling shortly."

Chapter 14

===================

The group gathered around the dining room table as Conner arrived from the guesthouse, or as Dexter called it, 'the situation room,' holding some papers.

"Last night the cruise ship *Infatuation* sunk off the Florida coast. The ship was hosting a conference of Cuban-American groups trying to decide the future of the island."

Tamargo, the only Cuban in the group shook his head. "The future of the island? What makes them expert in what's really happening in Cuba?"

Conner shrugged.

"Sounds like a meeting of Mafia bosses." Hawkins said.

Conner continued. "It has been leaked to the press that the ship's explosion and fire was an accident. At this time there are various reports circulating regarding the maintenance of the ship." Conner passed a picture of the ship followed by another picture.

"The first boat to respond to the cruise ship's distress call was the USS San Juan, a nuclear attack sub leaving Port Everglades. *San Juan,* as well as other warships was in South Florida as part of the Fleet Week Celebration."

"Did *San Juan* have anything to do with this?" Becker asked.

"In a way. *San Juan* was already on patrol; they had identified the cruise ship when something else appeared on their sonar." Conner passed a third picture. "This is an old Russian, Alpha Class, attack submarine. According to *San Juan*, *Infatuation* was sunk by an Alpha like the one in that picture."

"Steven," Becker interrupted. "I'm not too caught up in Russia's arsenal but weren't all Alpha class submarines retired by 2000?"

"Some even before that. We're currently checking on it but it seems that at least one of them managed to disappear."

"Considering the Russian's urgency for money, it wouldn't surprise me," commented Hawkins.

Becker nodded.

"The point is that the Cubans were aware of this meeting and they had the resources to neutralize it. We need to know what else they might have. If there's even a discrepancy in any of the Russian big ballistic submarines we might have a huge problem in our own back yard."

"Well, other than the submarine incident, it seems that they are not making any military moves. Satellite pictures indicate very little movement," Dexter said.

When you say little; do you mean unusual?" Becker asked.

"In comparison to previous months, a reduction of about 30%."

"Keep us posted if anything changes." Conner said as his cellular phone began to ring. "Jerry, what is it?" He pointed at the television and Becker reached for the remote. "Thanks, Jerry. I will call you back within the hour." Conner disconnected the call as Becker raised the volume on the TV.

"According to sources in Havana, the trials were conducted in private and the sentencings were announced just a few minutes ago."

"Trials?" Hawkins asked loudly.

"That's why we lost contact with most of them before the explosion. They were picked up, and now they're being blamed for what happened."

"All sixty seven were convicted of high treason and espionage; all but one will be facing a firing squad. It has been rumored that this will happen tomorrow morning after a press conference."

"Mute that," Conner said.

Becker pressed a button on the remote, silencing the TV reporter.

"Why carry out the sentencing so fast?" Hawkins asked.

"So that we don't respond in any way?" Becker replied.

"All right people, we need to take care of business." Conner's look changed, he seemed focus, making Becker smiled. "Hawkins, contact Kim Murray at the FBI office, we need her help on the cruise ship."

Hawkins looked confused.

"We need to know if someone from any of the Anti-Castro groups made any unusual calls to the island. Murray should be able to help."

Hawkins eyes widened. "You mean someone tipped the Cubans off."

"Probably.

Hawkins nodded in agreement.

"It might take time. Check the groups and the ship's agency. Anyone that might have been aware of the meeting."

The tall man straighten making Conner think that he would be saluted.

"Next, we need to make contact with the island once again. Loosing so many people only means that someone knew of this ahead of time. I know that one of these two men might be the one responsible for everything that's happening there, but we need to get more information."

The group nodded.

Conner turned to Dexter next.

"Be ready to send another strand of Minerva. We need to send a message to gather as much information as possible. He is to meet a contact very soon, I should have a date and time by late afternoon."

"If you ask me, I think we should send a team; some kind of special ops," Dexter said.

"They'll be expecting something like that," Conner replied. "We need to get information somehow and this is the only way."

Tamargo, who had kept silent throughout the meeting, raised his hand. "I would like to volunteer sir, that is if you still don't have someone in mind."

"Actually Tamargo, we don't. I put in a request to go myself, but so far Van Buren has not answered."

"In that case sir, I want to volunteer." Tamargo insisted.

"I'll take it under advisement. Remember, this might be a very dangerous mission."

"I know sir."

"Very well." Conner said picking up the papers. "Dismissed."

The group began to walk away, leaving Conner and Becker alone.

"There's something else, isn't there?" Becker asked.

Conner nodded, trying to avoid direct contact with her eyes.

"What is it?"

"The Russians aren't being very cooperative. They are keeping very quiet about the Alpha."

This time it was Becker who turned her eyes away.

Conner walked around the table and kneeled in front of her. "Look, I know this is too much to ask, but we're getting desperate. It's not only that submarine, we don't know what other surprises they might have."

Becker remained quiet, her eyes still looking directly at the floor.

"Ann—"

"I'll make the call," she said, her voice soft, almost a murmur.

"Ann," Conner whispered back. "It's only a suggestion. You don't have to."

Becker shook her head softly. "I understand. Right now it's the only option."

Conner agreed.

"Besides," she said softly. "You have made some tough decisions today."

Conner looked at Tamargo who was sitting by the pool talking to Dexter. "If it helps, I'm sorry."

Becker smiled back.

Chapter 15

====================

The park was now different, something Conner did not expect. He recalled the countless time when he would sit by the water, watching the waves hit the rock. The water gave him a soothing feeling, letting his mind relax and slowly work on the problems he was having. That was the reason he was here now. His mind however was still in the conversation he had with Becker.

She needed time, he thought.

The park was different; he noticed it the moment he drove in. A basketball court and playground were now part of a new fenced area; new benches were also added.

As he watched the waves crashed against the rocks Conner looked around him once again. It was hard to describe how a place he knew so well had changed so much, a place almost alien to him.

Conner closed his eyes, leaving behind what he had seen and returning his mind to the place he once knew; the sounds were the same, the smell was the same. Within minutes Conner began to relax. It was a hard decision, sending Tamargo to what seemed to be a trap. It was even harder to send someone else; someone who had no idea how dangerous this was going to be; someone who lacked the training and the knowledge; a civilian. Without notice, Conner's mind made one small observation, *"yes, I've changed as well."*

Back in his car still, Conner made his first phone call. The voice of a woman answered almost immediately.

"Murray, it's Conner. I need a favor." He turned the engine and the car came to live. "I know you have contacts with some of those travel agencies that sell trips to Cuba."

Murray confirmed his comment.

"I need to get someone into the island. No, this is not official; it's a friend of the family that needs to desperately visit before all flights are cancelled. I don't want to get involved because I don't want to endanger his live." He frowned wondering if it was a good enough excuse.

Murray assured him she would take care of it.

"Kim, please keep this between us. Nobody else is to know."

Again, Conner received assurance.

"Thanks, I owe you." He was about to disconnect when he rapidly called out to her. "I nearly forgot. You will get a call from Hawkins soon. He wants to get together to go over something. I'll let him handle the details."

Conner hung up the phone and dialed another number. Dexter answered it.

"Dex, I need you to find a friend of mine. Name is Lt. Colonel Kristopher James, US Navy. When you find him, give him my number and tell him that he owes me a racquetball game."

Not waiting for a reply, Conner severed the connection and dialed another number.

"Operator, I need the number for Peirama Games."

Juan Navarro looked at the clock on the wall once again, 1:00 PM. He felt anxious, wondering why were they taking so long. The virus arrived the previous day early in the morning and he answered it almost immediately, yet there was no response. He spent the entire day by the computer, waiting for some kind of message. If the Americans were in such need of information, why haven't they contacted him?

Conner returned to the house refreshed. As before, his time in the old park had the exact effect it did in the past. Conner thought of taking Becker to the park, show her the one place that he could always returned to. "*Soon,*" he though. *Now, we have work to do.*

Conner noticed Becker in the pool but he continued walking toward the guesthouse. She made no attempt to follow him, nor call him. Conner knew this was not an easy task he'd asked of her.

"What do you have?" He asked Dexter.

The man turned around and gave him a small package. "Tamargo's passport, papers, and round tickets for Havana on June 28th"

"Great!" Conner said.

"I have Minerva ready; all we need is a message."

"Can you send a small picture?" Conner asked.

"Sure, I'll send a small resolution picture. What do you have in mind?"

"Tamargo's face," Conner said without pausing.

Dexter did not ask any questions, turning and typing a few commands. A passport-like picture of Tamargo appeared on the screen. "Good enough?"

"Yes," Conner said.

Dexter opened a program and made some changes to the picture. When completed, the size of the file was reduced by 80 percent.

"Type this message," Conner said.

"Ready!"

"Antonio Tamargo, arriving from Miami on June 28th. Please give him as much information as you can."

"Got it!" Dexter said.

"Hold it!" Conner stopped him from sending the file. "Add 'desperately need help!'"

Dexter typed the information and paused. "Anything else."

Conner shook his head. "No, send it."

Dexter pressed a button and the file disappeared from the screen.

Conner's eyes remained on the blank screen. *I might have just signed Tamargo's death certificate.*

Eduardo Peralta acknowledged the message he had received via the new strand of the Minerva virus. He was worried that someone would see it, since a group of coworkers were having a heated conversation next to his desk. He typed his code word and immediately sent the virus back. He turned his attention back to the group, assuring himself that they did not notice.

Waiting for the crowd to disperse, Peralta got up and walked to the only phone on his floor.

"It's me," he said to the voice on the other end. "I received a message."

"What did they say?" the man on the other end asked.

"They have someone coming on the 28th of June. I am to meet him, name is Antonio Tamargo."

"Good. We have been tracking for any type of unusual activity. The virus came in directly to your section."

"Meaning?" Peralta said confused.

"Meaning that you are the only one they contacted."

Peralta smiled. "They seemed desperate."

"I'm sure they are. That is why you are going to show Mr. Tamargo everything he asks." The voice on the phone seemed friendly but stern.

"Don't worry sir, I already have pages worth of information."

Chapter 16

=================

Juan Navarro arrived at his home disappointed. He spent the entire day nervously waiting for communication, a message, something. As the day came to a closing he knew that the message was long overdue. He was not sure if they had passed him once again as non-essential or if they had given him up as a risk.

He recalled better days, when countless times he provided valuable information, risking his life for a cause he thought was just. But that was long ago.

"Face it Juan, you're too old for this." He had barely uttered the words when the phone began to ring.

"Oigo?"

"Juan? It's your aunt Barbara," the voice of a woman answered back. "How are you mi hijito?"

Navarro paused slightly. He had an aunt name Barbara living in the states. She had visited the island a few times and had even visited his house. The call, however, felt strange.

"I'm calling you because I need a favor from you."

"Yes, of course," Navarro answered still confused.

"My best friend's son, Miguel, is going to Cuba on June 20th. He's only planning to be there for three days but I promised his mother that he could count on you. I'm sure you remember her, Georgina DeVera."

Navarro's confusion turned to shock. This was a name Navarro knew well, a name he had not heard in years, but immediately got Navarro's attention. DeVera was the woman who brought him into the struggle, the one who trained him and taught him everything he knew. "Yes, I remember her," he finally mumbled.

"Although he IS NOT family; I want you to treat him as such."

"Not family?" Navarro asked himself.

"I'm sending a few things for you since he's not taking too much luggage," the voice continued. "The reason he is going to the island is to visit some of the places where his father grew up. According to Miguel, he promised this to his father before he died."

Navarro's mind was now alert, every word being carefully scrutinized.

Barbara continued. "He has a few cousins and uncles that he might want to visit; but you can determine if you can take him or not. I know you're the only one with a car but I don't know what your situation is with gas and such."

"No, it's fine. I'll ask for a few days off at work."

"Thank you. Please send me some letters; I really want to know how everyone is doing..."

Barbara was now being more than obvious but Navarro needed some kind of confirmation. He needed to make sure; and immediately thought what to say. "Tia, did you receive the cigar I sent to Uncle Ramon?"

There was a small pause making Juan swear that the communication had been lost. He was mistaken.

"Yes we did, thank you."

"How about cousin Carmen? I know she was kind of worried about taking cigars from Cuba to the US."

The pause was longer this time forcing Navarro to speak. "Tia?"

"I don't know how to tell you this. Your cousin died."

"Died? How?"

"Car accident," his aunt said. "We never saw her after she returned from Cuba."

Navarro was speechless.

"I'll send you a letter with the details. I'm sure you want to know all about it, since she always talked about you so much."

Navarro's eyes changed swiftly. At first he felt his vision cloud up, a sudden sign of weakness that he immediately put aside. If what they said was true, Marcie never made contact; someone must have

found her. This wasn't the time for grief; this was the time for action.
"When is he arriving?" he asked steadying himself.

"June 20th. He's pretty young, around 25-26, always wearing
jeans."

"I'll be there."

"Thanks, I knew I could count on you." Please remember; he's
not family but he's the son of a good friend. Drive him to see his
family and his father's old home, that's why he's going. The rest,
although important for me, could wait until he is about to leave."

"Okay." Navarro said.

"Oh, another thing. Don't tell anyone that I called. If the girls
find out that I'll be sending something, they will be calling and asking
for things. Don't tell anyone, you know how they get."

"You don't have to tell me." Navarro said.

"Seriously, don't let anyone know. I don't want a whole family
fight because I called you and not them."

"You know them so well" Navarro said amused.

"Listen, I have to go. I'm sending you a nice little gift with
Miguel."

"Don't worry tia, I'll be there."

"Thank you, Juan."

Navarro hung up the phone; his mind racing. There were a few
things he wasn't sure but he would figure them out soon enough. He
knew that they needed information and according to the date, they
needed it soon. The other piece of information was obvious to him;
there was a double agent. He was told more than once not to trust
anyone.

There was only one thing that bothered him, the contact. He
wasn't sure if he understood, but according to what they said it seems
that the contact was a civilian.

Back in Homestead, three computer screens in the guestroom
house were still bursting with activity. One screen was showing a
location in a map. The location was labeled 'Barbara Garcia's
Home', Juan Navarro's aunt. Above, readouts showed a severed
communication between the Garcia's house and a long distance
carrier. The connection between her house and the guestroom house
was still open.

"Terminating connection," Dexter said typing a few commands.

"So?" the voice asked through the computer speakers, its face
showing in one of the monitors.

"Hold on," Dexter said typing another command. "Okay, say something."

"Something," the voice said, this time sounding less like an old lady and more like the twenty-something woman on the screen.

"Rosie, you're a natural," Conner said smiling at the tiny camera watching him from above the monitor.

"Thanks. Anything else you guys need?" she asked.

"No, that's all. Thank you kiddo," Conner replied.

"Well, you guys have a good night down there in BEAUTIFUL Miami," she said almost pouting.

Conner smiled again. "Hey Rosie, maybe you want to join us down here."

"Sure!" she shouted.

"I'll call you," he said disconnecting the line.

"That was mean," Dexter said.

Conner looked back at him. "No, when all this is over, I'll make sure she takes a nice vacation down here. Meanwhile, I don't want anyone else knowing about this. Is that understood?"

Dexter nodded seriously.

"I mean it Dexter. This little information is between you and me."

Dexter began to speak but was soon silent by the picture on one of the screens. A news reporter was speaking rapidly while a red 'Breaking News' banner continued to flash under a smaller one, reading 'Live: Havana, Cuba.'

The camera moved frantically back and forth until it finally stopped on an old, old building. The picture was grainy and dark, as the camera zoomed closer to the balcony.

Conner, already watching, moved closer to the screen. "Do you have audio on this?"

Dexter began to fumble for the remote. "Audio? Oh, yes."

The volume bar began to increase; yet the sound was not apparent. There was no reporter talking; only the hushed sound of a crowd gathering around the camera.

Slowly, from the darkness, a figure began to emerge; an imposing figure that finally stood in front of the balcony as the crowd around the camera began to cheer.

"Holly shit! You were right. It was him all along." Dexter continued to watch the screen as the face of Fidel Castro finally came into the light.

Conner wasn't surprised. He had waited to see the face for over a week. "It's about time," he said turning around and walking away.

Chapter 17

==================

"Mr. Conner," the voice of the Secretary of Defense seemed cool and calculating as the old man shook his hand. "I must say that it is hard for me to admit when I'm wrong; however I do have to say that you prove me wrong in many ways."

The man continued to keep a firm handshake on Conner.

"Still," Conner said not releasing his own grip. "Sir I do owe you an apology." He felt the man's grip releasing his hand slightly. "No matter how much I believe in what I was saying, I should've—"

"That's not important now," the Secretary of Defense interrupted finally releasing the handshake. "If you are the future, as Van Buren puts it, you do need to learn to be a politician as well."

"Yes, sir." Conner felt the man's arm on his shoulder as the doors to the conference room opened.

She had no reason to be mad at this man; she had no real reason to be mad at all. Every time she had to call Dimitri Novloskov she felt uneasy, scared. But the feeling normally disappeared after she met him. This time was no different, except for what she found out.

Dimitri called her the day before with news. He told her that the news were important and refused to provide her any information over the phone. She tried to persuade him, but he insisted until she arranged a meeting outside the Smithsonian National Air and Space Museum in the National Mall.

She waited for Conner to leave before she called for a cab. Her flight was leaving only an hour after his, but she wanted to do this on her own.

Becker knew Novloskov well and immediately sat on the first bench she found. There was no sense in looking for him; he will find her. He knew how to do this better than her; he had been doing it for over thirty years. Now a diplomat, the ex-KGB agent found her immediately.

What he had to say was not encouraging.

"First, the good news." He said after kissing her softly on the cheek.

Becker realized that he was in a hurry. Whether it was true or his way of making her feel better she did not know, but she appreciated it.

"The Alpha was Cuban. Prior to decommissioning all Alphas, there was a request from the Cuban government. Delivery was made on November of last year. They have no other submarines. You have my word."

Becker's face remained unchanged.

"I also have information regarding missiles. This is where the bad news begin."

"I'm sorry, I don't understand."

"The Cubans have been desperately looking into purchasing ICBMs. They have made inquiries not only to us, but also to the Chinese. I could assure you that they have no ICBMs as of yet."

"Okay," Becker said. She tried not to show her relief. An Inter Continental Ballistic Missile would give Cuba the means to destroy a city anywhere in the United States.

Novloskov seemed rushed. "It appears that the Chinese felt as uneasy as we did about selling these weapons to the Cubans."

"That's a relief," Becker added.

"Of course the only reason they did not sell them is probably because the Cubans could reach them as easily as any other country they would choose." He smiled back at her.

"But?" Becker asked. "I know there's a but."

"Yes, there is."

"Go on."

"It appears that the Cubans have acquired two 50-kiloton nuclear warheads."

"Are you sure about this?"

"Yes, it has been confirmed, I believe your classification is AA60 Tactical Nuclear Warhead." He tried to smile but her face remained the same. "I'm sorry."

"I'm sure we can get this information but do you have any idea the type of missiles they will be using? Type of range?" Becker asked.

"I don't know what type of missiles the Cubans have at this time, but let's just say that the southeast coast of the US will be in grave danger."

She saw the faces of many people she knew, all flashing before her eyes. *Conner!*

"One more thing," Novloskov said. "Someone in your NAS is feeding the Cuban information."

"What type of information?" she asked startling herself.

"Satellite positions. They know the times, they are working around it."

Ann said nothing; her mind was trying to process all the information. She noticed his eyes, staring at her.

"What?" Becker said uncomfortable.

"I'm looking at what an amazing woman you have become."

She stopped herself from smiling.

"Ilyana," he said softly.

"It's Ann."

"I know, Ann." He struggled with the name. "I wish your mother could see you now, the big American CIA."

"Dad!" she said firmly.

"It's ironic, the fact that my daughter—"

"Don't start," she said. "I don't even know how they even accepted me."

"Because, my child, you are an asset. Who else could have gathered all this information but you?"

She looked at him, for the first time she realized how old he had become. "And yet they trust me."

"Of course, we are not the mortal enemies we once were, and even then. You are not the first one you know."

"I have a question. Why did they give you all this information?"

"Because. Castro has many friends in Russia; but he has made many more enemies."

"Of course," she replied.

"I have a question for you. Why do you hate me so much?"

The question hit her hard. It was something she was not expecting. "I don't—"

"Please," he interrupted. "Although I must admit you seem more, what's the word, friendly? Perhaps this man, Conner? Perhaps he was smart in making you call me."

"How did you—?" Becker stopped herself knowing better than to ask. "Never mind."

Novloskov's eyes widened. "What's that a smile?"

She tried to conceal it but was unsuccessful.

"I'll make you a deal, dad. If you are right with this information, I'll treat you to a large dinner anywhere you'll like."

"One condition." Novloskov arm reached for her and Becker welcomed the embrace. "I want to meet this Conner."

"Deal!"

For the first time since she could remember, Ann Becker hugged her father good-bye.

Steven Conner could not help but smile. Although the Secretary of Defense seemed to be questioning some of his points, the man seemed honestly interested in what he had to say. It was something Conner welcome since both the National Security Advisor and the Chairman of the Joint Chiefs were almost in complete agreement with him. Van Buren, however, remained silent, not showing any emotions.

"Mr. Conner," the Secretary of Defense continued. "Let me see if I understand. You want us to play possum and let the Cubans believe we are unaware of their intentions."

"Yes, sir. If we show any hint that we're on to them, they might back down on their plans."

"And this is bad, why?"

"Because if they continue to follow this plan we will be ready. We have found a pattern; one that we believe is the key to all the recent attacks. A plan that will culminate in one particular date, the most important date in Castro's Cuba."

"July 26th of course." The Secretary answered.

Conner did not seem interested in the Secretary's knowledge. Without even acknowledging the man's answer, he continued. "If they follow this pattern, we will be prepared, that is if you all approve my plan. If we allow the Cubans to know that we are on to them, they might change the date, leaving us open to be attacked at any time."

"I see, but with this evidence we can expose their plans. Or even better, why not attack them first?" The Secretary's voice had a hint of sarcasm.

"Mr. Secretary, an attack is out of the question. If we do such a thing the whole world will side with Castro as he will play the victim once again."

"This might be what he is really after."

Touché', Conner thought. "That could be correct sir, however I think Castro is in no mood to play games with us. I think this is a plan that he always had, and for some reason he is finally executing it."

"But why?"

"I don't know sir; maybe he's sick or dying. Maybe he noticed Marcano's popularity and realized that he is losing his power."

"Or maybe he wants to play with us once again," the Secretary concluded. "Still, you have not answered why we can't just expose him."

"Because, as you said sir, if he is playing with us, this will be exactly what he would expect us to do. But if we do, he will simply deny it and find a way to turn it to his favor as he has done many times."

Conner paused, allowing the statement to sink in. "Since I don't believe this is his plan I would have to say that it would be a bad idea to try to expose him." Conner did not wait for a reply. "Again, he will play the victim, accusing us of whatever he can think of while changing or canceling the attack altogether. We might be able to stop him from attacking us now but we will never know if he will attack us later."

The Secretary of Defense remained quiet, his eyes studying Conner carefully.

"All I ask is for us to be prepared. We need to be able to defend Guantanamo from a full-scale attack. We also need to keep vigilant, since an attack might be planned for Miami as well."

"And your suggestion," the Chairman of the Joint Chiefs interrupted. "Is for us to let the Cubans think we are unaware of what is happening while we prepare for an attack."

"Yes sir."

The man's face remained unchanged. "I think we can handle that."

"That's all I ask." Conner said opening his briefcase. He removed multiple packages and passed it to each of the men around the table. "I have outlined some of the points that need your attention." Conner felt a vibration coming from his cell phone. Ignoring it, he continued. "Gentlemen,

The vibration changed to a high-pitched alarm, something that took both Conner and Van Buren by surprised. Both men placed their phones on 'vibrate' before beginning the meeting; the alarm was a feature that was only used for emergencies.

Conner picked up the phone immediately, surprised that Van Buren's phone did not ring at all. "Becker? What is it?"

Conner moved away from the conference as Becker relayed the message she received from Novloskov.

Hanging up the phone, Conner returned to the table, his face not truly showing what he had heard.

"Mr. Conner, I feel that I speak for anyone when I said that we agree with you wholeheartedly." The Joint Chief said.

Everyone around the table nodded.

"I would like to ask, with Van Buren's permissions of course, for you to remain available to us, in case we need to reach you at a given time."

Van Buren said nothing, his eyes fixed on Conner.

"I'm sorry to interrupt sir, but I think everyone here should be informed of the news I just received."

Chapter 18

=================

Colonel Rogelio Berrios walked into the dark apartment. He used the spare set of keys to let himself in, wanting to surprise his mistress when she arrived. Berrios entire week had been exhausting and he needed some relaxation.

She should be home soon Berrios thought sitting on the old rocking chair that he bought for himself last year. He didn't even bother to turn on the light, closing his eyes as his body relaxed.

"*Coronel* Berrios!" the voice was deep and harsh.

Berrios jumped from the chair and went for his sidearm, only to find it missing.

"Is this what you're looking for?" the voice said from the shadows, the gun slightly visible.

"Who are you? What do you want?" He asked sounding shaky. "What did you do with Margarita?"

"I don't know where she is, I'm here for you."

"For me?" the voice was beginning to crack.

"We had a mutual friend, Maria Cecilia Fernandez." The voice said. "Please sit down; I'm not going to hurt you."

Berrios was still not convinced. He moved a step forward, then another. "If you mean what you said…"

In response, the man moved forward as well. "Here," Navarro said giving him the gun. "To show you good faith."

Berrios took the gun trying to see the face of the man standing in front of him. He was not successful. Whoever this man was, he knew enough to cover his face with some kind of mask. "Who are you?" Berrios asked again putting his gun back in the holster.

"My name is not important," Navarro said. "Let's just say I'm an old friend of Marcie."

"And that's supposed to mean something to me?" Berrios asked.

Navarro kept his cool, at least for the moment. "Look Colonel, I know you were passing information to her."

"Me? Passing information to someone, that's—"

"Marcie's dead!" Navarro exploded. "I need to know what else did you tell her to get her killed."

Berrios fell on the sofa. "She's dead? How?"

"I don't know," Navarro replied. "She paid me a visit the night before she left. She said that you had given her really important information."

"Yes, yes. I recalled that she came to see me, said something about making arrangements to leave."

"I know. Did she tell you who was making the arrangements?"

"No," Berrios said.

Navarro wasn't convinced. "Colonel, I need you to think. It's important."

Berrios thought for a moment, shaking his head slightly. "I'm sorry."

Navarro began to walk away.

"Wait, once she mentioned a man by the name of Peralta. Something about him helping her get some people out of the island."

"Peralta," Navarro said. "It's a start."

"Did you know her long?" Berrios asked.

Navarro nodded slightly.

She was barely 19 when he saw her for the first time, smashing the car window of a Foreign Interest Section member. He grabbed her hand as it came down once again against the window. She tried to flee, but he didn't let her. He dragged her into the shadows as two militia soldiers came running.

At first she fought him, but he held her, kept her in the shadows, hidden from certain prison. By the time the two soldiers left, she was no longer struggling.

"Why didn't you let me finish it?" she asked that night.

"Because," he replied. "You need to learn how to pick your fights."

"I'm sorry," Berrios said.

"Me too." Navarro's voice was once again deep and businesslike. "I do have some questions for you."

"Yes, anything I can do to help."

"You can begin by telling me what was so important that had her killed."

Chapter 19

===============

Michael Lopez felt edgy as he continued to look out the window; his mind racing while he pretended to watch the workers load the plane.

"Excuse me," a man said standing in the aisle by Lopez' row.

"Oh, I'm sorry," Lopez, said moving his laptop from the adjacent seat.

"Would you like me to put it on the overhead for you?" the man asked.

"No thanks; I'm planning to work during the flight."

The man smiled crookedly. "To Cuba? You'll be landing by the time you turn it on." He sat on the chair and extended his hand. "Ignacio Gutierrez"

"Michael Lopez."

"Business trip?" Gutierrez asked.

"No, actually I'm on a pilgrimage of sort."

"A pilgrimage?"

"My father always wanted me to visit; find my roots if you will."

"Oh, I see."

"When he died last month; I figured that I owe it to him."

"Oh, I'm sorry."

Lopez nodded.

"But if you are on this…pilgrimage; why are you bringing your work with you."

"I have to; deadlines you know."

The man was friendly enough and Michael found himself enjoying the conversation; barely noticing the plane taking off. Soon enough he disengaged himself from the conversation and turned on his laptop.

The screen came to life and after a few strokes Michael Lopez began to type a string of numbers and letters.

"I'm sorry; what exactly is that?" Gutierrez asked.

"This?" Michael pointed at the screen. "Computer coding; I'm a game designer."

"You make games? Really?"

"Ever heard of 'Peirama'?"

"No, sorry."

"Oh, it's okay, it's an old game, well in computer term that is. I also worked on 'Black Iris'."

The man shook his head.

Lopez smiled, "How about 'Zenith Fire'?"

"I know that one, military game right?"

"Yeah, that's the one."

"Game of the year right?"

"Yup, two years ago." Lopez began to type once again. "Unfortunately it's not so much what you did, but what you can do now."

Gutierrez continued to watch Lopez entering codes. "How do you know what you are doing?"

"Well, I'm currently creating a scene for one of the levels." He typed a command and a large room appeared on the screen. "See this room?"

Gutierrez nodded.

Lopez returned to the data section and changed a few numbers. Once again he returned to the room; now painted in neon colors.

"The colors changed!" Gutierrez exclaimed.

Lopez nodded. "There are different ways to do it; I'm fixing some codes before the engine is…" Lopez noticed the man, his eyes fixed on the screen. "Here," he said changing the screen. "This is how it looks on the previous level."

The scene was a field; blades of glass flowing with the wind as creatures walked slowly nearby.

"That is amazing!"

"I hope my boss feels the same way when I show him this."

"I'm sure he will like it very much."

"Thanks."

Conner watched from the large glass window as the plane began to take off. He closed his eyes and said a small prayer for the man. He was not a religious man, but they needed all the help they could get.

He was afraid of sending anyone, especially a civilian, but at the time he had no choice. Selecting Tamargo for the mission was dangerous, but Tamargo knew the danger it was part of his job. Lopez, on the other hand, had no formal training. True, he did this type of job once before, but this was different; this time it was dangerous. Unfortunately, Conner felt that he had no choice. Lopez was excellent with computers and the perfect person to move data in and out of the island.

"Godspeed," Conner said as the plane disappeared from view.

There was something else that bothered him, something that he chose to ignore. He noticed the man boarding the plane right before the gate closed. He recognized him as the one responsible for the assassination of the INS agent. The man that Henderson and his team were desperately looking for. He saw him board the plane but made no attempt to stop him. He couldn't, the stakes were too high.

Conner checked his watch again and got up to leave. He looked back at the skies one last time before he walked away.

Chapter 20

==================

Michael Lopez was confused; he had no one to help him understand. He was neither a spy, nor an agent in any way. His cover was not much of a cover; it was a fact.

He had come to Cuba for the same reasons he told the family members that continued to visit him; to visit his father's birthplace. Meeting them was secondary; he was only here to see where his father grew up.

He knew he was approached because of a job he did once before, a 'game' he created four years ago for the NSA. What he didn't understand was why? How could the US be so desperate to hire him to do this type of work?

Steven Conner approached him days before as he prepared for his trip to Cuba. At the time he thought the man was joking, playing with him. It was only after Conner explained the severity of the situation that he realized how important this visit was. It was also then that Michael Lopez realized why it had been so easy for him to get passage to the island. A trip that was impossible to make, especially now that all visits to the island would be cancelled after July 1st.

Conner explained to him that he will be contacted by a friend of the family, someone who might be able to drive him around. Lopez was not to do anything but wait. Once the contact was made, his only job was to transport the information provided to him in the safest way possible.

Conner guaranteed that he would not be under any danger. The contact would take Lopez to meet his family, as well as any place that he wished. There was one safeguard, Conner said. If the contact would drive him to relatives that Lopez had no knowledge of; it would be an indication that they were being watched.

That never happened.

Lopez spent the first day visiting family. He knew it would be inappropriate for him to arrive at the island and not visit his family. What he didn't expect was the outpour of love from family and friends he never met before. Within a few hours, the house was full of people he had never met, people that were telling him stories of his father. People who were willing to share anything they could with him, a total stranger.

It was here where he realized that walking the same streets that his father walked wasn't as important as sharing all the memories with people who knew him.

The second day he was driven near the house where his father grew up. The man stopped the car a block away and turned off the engine.

"Why are we stopping here?" Lopez asked.

"You say you wanted to see your father's place, walked were he walked. The address is roughly a block away."

Michael Lopez understood. He opened the door and stepped out of the car. "Thank you," he said softly.

Juan Navarro watched the man walked slowly down the street, touching the walls, looking all around him. A hint of shame hit Navarro as he watched Lopez moved closer to the address he came to visit. Once, this had been a beautiful neighborhood, its building showing with pride the architectural marvel they once were.

In contrast, the buildings were now falling apart, the paint, if there was any, peeling away and faded. Navarro wondered if they were still safe to live in. He heard a few days ago about a building that had just collapse; of course it was never in any news report.

The street was empty but Navarro could not help himself, it was in his blood. He had been extra careful, looking behind his shoulder more than usual, just like he was doing now.

"Nada," he said slightly disappointed.

He noticed that Lopez had stopped and was now kneeling by the sidewalk. Navarro wondered what the man was looking at but decided to stay where he was.

The sidewalk was broken in so many places that the surface looked like a map with roads leading to different locations. Michael's eyes were fixed in a small area of the sidewalk, an area probably ignored by everyone walking by each day.

A.L.

He knew immediately this was his father.

It was long ago, Michael barely remembered, when he and his brother signed their name on fresh cement somewhere on the side of the house. He recalled his father saying that he had done that as well, a long time ago, when he was a kid.

He traced the letters with his fingers again and again.

"Hello?" a woman's voice said from the window beside him.

"Oh, I'm sorry," Lopez said.

"You're from the states aren't you?"

"Yes, I am." Lopez stood up feeling embarrassed. "I'm just visiting the neighborhood."

"I don't recall seeing you before, and I've lived here all my life," the woman asked.

"No, not me. My father grew up in this neighborhood."

"Your father lived around here?"

"Yes ma'am. He lived in the apartment next door."

"Next door? Oh, come on in son, I know the person that lives there. Eloisa will be more than happy to show you the apartment."

"Oh I don't want to bother."

"It's no bother. Come in, Come in!"

Chapter 21

====================

"Well here they are; the last pictures before we lost the satellite." Raul Castro announced, tossing the package on his brother's desk.

General Guerra saluted at the younger Castro and began to leave.

"This concerns you too Guerra," Fidel Castro said.

"*Si, mi comandante*." Guerra replied.

"So what excuse did the Russians give you this time?" Fidel asked.

"They feel that we're playing a very dangerous game and they don't want to be involved."

"It seems that our old friends have lost their backbone after all." Fidel Castro said lighting a cigar.

His brother's eyes watched him and the cigar almost in protest.

Fidel returned the look making the younger Castro remain silent. Once sure that Raul would not make a comment about his cigar, Fidel continued. "We should've forced them to give us at least one or two more satellites back in the good old days."

"I think that we would've been in the same situation," Raul said. "One of the reasons they are not allowing us to use it anymore is because they seem to have lost another one."

"Russian technology," Fidel said smiling at Guerra. He opened the package and started examining each photograph. "I see that there's still no activity in any of the military airports, and Miami is still going about their business.

"Like I told you, my brother, we have plugged every leak. Even better, the agent they are sending will leave satisfied."

The two men looked at Guerra who seemed confused.

"My brother," Raul said. "Don't you think is time we can bring our General up to speed?"

"Yes Raul," Fidel said standing up and walking around his oak desk. "I think it's time."

The car squeaked and bounced as Navarro took another pothole a little too fast.

"Sorry," he apologized once again.

"No problem." Michael Lopez was trying to figure out what had gone wrong. Although there had been no hint of trouble; he was now on his way to the airport; leaving the island without any information.

"Do you want to stop for a beer before we get to the airport?"

"Well, I don't really drink," Lopez replied.

"A short stop? Si?" Navarro suggested, stopping the car in front of his house. As he opened the door to his car he turned to Lopez. "You better bring down your briefcase; the neighborhood is not too safe."

The two men entered the house and Navarro immediately pulled two beers from the refrigerator.

"Thanks," Lopez said taking a sip from the bottle. The beer, if it could be called that, had a taste unlike anything he's ever tasted. He was being honest before, he wasn't much of a drinker but Michael Lopez felt it would be impolite to refuse it.

Navarro excused himself and walked into his bedroom. He returned shortly with a set of papers. "Here you are," he said. I don't know how you are planning to pass this."

Lopez suddenly felt nervous. "What exactly is in here?"

"Few documents, pictures, and a couple of maps."

"How many pages?"

"Roughly 12 or 13, why?"

Lopez opened his bag and retrieved his laptop. As the computer began to boot up, he retrieved a digital camera as well. He placed the paper on the kitchen counter and took the first picture. After ensuring that the information was clear enough for someone to read it he continued taking the pictures without hesitation.

He connected the camera to his laptop and began to download the pictures. *So much for high-tech gadgets,* Lopez thought. He began to type some codes, quickly opening a program.

"How are you planning to hide those files?" Navarro asked.

"Sorry," Lopez said remembering a spy movie he'd watched recently. "Need to know."

Navarro laughed loudly and took another gulped of his beer. He knew the man had no formal training, but he was impressed.

Lopez ignored him as his fingers danced on the keyboard.

"Really, what are you doing?" Navarro asked again.

"I'm saving the files within a program; hiding them so that only I could find them. It's called an 'Easter Egg'."

Navarro nodded not fully understanding what the young man was trying to tell him.

"Here," Lopez said giving him the papers back.

Navarro grabbed the papers and placed it in a pot. He picked up a match and after lighting it up he began to burn the papers.

Michael eyes returned to his task. The file was now safe inside the game, making it impossible for anyone to find it. He deleted the pictures and began to make a backup copy of the game. *Just in case,* he thought.

Navarro burned the last piece of paper and turned to Lopez who was now closing his laptop. "Ready?"

"Not yet." Lopez said removing a diskette from his pocket. He handed the disk to Navarro who immediately asked.

"What's this?"

"Someone promised you more information regarding a mutual friend. I was told to give it to you. I presume you have a computer."

Navarro nodded. "Thank you." He smiled at the young man, who once again seemed nervous. "I never met your father; I don't even know who he was but I'm sure that he was an exceptional man and he would be very proud."

"It's funny, I thought this trip would be just to keep a promise but in such a short time I've learned so much about him."

Navarro raised his bottle. "To our fathers, wherever they are."

"To our fathers!"

Chapter 22

===================

Kristopher James stood between the two yellow lines letting the small ball drop to the floor. As it bounced back to hip level, he swung his racket at full strength and watched as the ball smashed into the wall. The little rubber ball bounced back as it left a powdery blue coloring on the gray walls.

The ball went straight for Conner's head, and he shifted to the side, dodging it by an inch.

"That was a good dodge Conner," James said grabbing the ball as he reached him. "I believe that makes it my game."

Conner said nothing, concentrating instead on catching his breath.

"So are you finally going to tell me what this is about or did you fly me all the way here so you could lose in racquetball?"

Conner was still crouched by the corner, beads of sweat rolling from his forehead. He looked at his shirt in contrast to James'. "Don't you even sweat?"

"Playing racquetball? Against you?"

Conner smiled. "We have a job for you, but this one is not going to be easy."

"When is it? That job in Ecuador left two of my guys in the hospital for almost three months."

"I know, and I'm sorry."

"Part of the business."

"I'm afraid, this one might be worse."

"Cuba?" James asked.

Conner kicked the can as he let his legs stretch. "Why Cuba? Why not Afghanistan, Iran, somewhere—"

"Don't insult my intelligence Conner."

"Your team should preferably speak Spanish."

"Cuba? Great!" James said with a hint of cynicism. "The pearl of the Caribbean, yet every time we've infiltrated that hellish island we screw something up. What type of recon?"

"I'm afraid this is not a recon mission. "I can't tell you much; I have very limited information so far."

"Okay, fine." James said in disgust. "Time frame?"

"Less than a month." Conner noticed the other man's look. "We have a place for you at Homestead."

James changed the ball to his other hand. "Training?"

"You have two choices. There's an area on the actual base but I'm sure you might be more interested in our old training facility in the Everglades."

"Been there, can't say I was impressed."

"You should see it now."

"At least throw me a bone, who's our target."

Conner knew that he owed the man some information. "Not who, but what. We need you to infiltrate and secure a heavily guarded area."

James remained silent for a moment, his mind racing quickly.

"Anybody I want?"

"Anybody."

"Weapons?"

"Anything you need."

"Fine. Call me tomorrow so that we can arrange a few transfers."

"Done!" Conner said reaching the door.

"Let's hope this time we have better communication." James said walking away.

"Damn it Kris," Conner grunted between his teeth.

Chapter 23

==================

"What is this?" the man in the olive uniform asked grabbing Michael Lopez' laptop.

"It's my computer, it's my work."

"I can't allow you to take this. How do I know you're not a spy?"

"You can turn the damn thing on and we can check it one file at a time," Michael said more annoyed than nervous.

"Maybe we should," the man replied moving the laptop to an empty table nearby.

Lopez' anger was evident in his face. He knew this was a way for the guard to get a few extra dollars, or a slightly used laptop computer.

"Look, I'm sure there's something we could do," he said noticing the computer was already being powered on. "Okay, fine. Let's do it your way."

A second guard arrived and after moving Lopez' bag, began to inspect it once again.

"What's this?" he asked, pulling a compact disc from the bag.

"It's my work;" Lopez replied clenching his teeth.

"You need to leave this behind."

"Over my dead body!" Lopez shouted realizing all too late that he was letting them get to him. "Look, this is my work; I have hundreds of hours worth of work in that disc."

He moved slightly closer. "Check it out; put it in the computer."

"Give me that," the other guard said taking the disc away from the man. He placed the disc on the tray and closed it. A black screen appeared.

"Press the 'Ctrl' & 'Alt' keys."

The man pressed the keys but nothing happened.

"No, hold one and then the other."

As soon as the keys were pressed the screen changed to a vast field surrounded by snow peaked mountains.

"It's a game. I'm a game designer."

The first soldier nodded while the second one stood motionless watching the screen."

"If you press this key right here," Lopez said pressing the 'up' arrow. Immediately the figure of a soldier appeared and began to move forward.

Lopez turned to see that the line near him was slowly thinning yet the guard show no sign of finishing with him. "Is there any way we can finish this soon?"

The guards ignored him making Lopez annoyance raise another level.

"Maybe we should keep it," the second guard said.

"What's going on here?" the voice from behind Lopez boomed.

As the two soldiers stood in attention Lopez turned to see the newly arrived soldier.

"Mr. Gutierrez?"

"Actually is Lieutenant Gutierrez."

"Oh, I didn't know," Lopez said feeling a slight hint of hesitation.

"Are these men harassing you?"

"Oh, no" Lopez said glancing at the two men that were now looking more nervous than him. "We were merely discussing the value of my laptop."

"Is that so?"

Michael nodded. *"That'll teach you assholes."*

"Put that back immediately!" Gutierrez said

"Yes sir!"

The two men rushed to put everything back in order. Lopez pretended to ignore them.

"I was hoping to see you on the plane," Lopez said to Gutierrez. "I guess you're not returning with us."

"No, I have business here at home."

"Oh," Lopez said disappointed. "I was planning to show you some of the new stuff I designed while I was here."

"Perhaps another time. How did your...pilgrimage go?" Gutierrez asked.

"Actually, I learned a lot from the people that knew my father when he was young." Lopez removed his digital camera and turned the power on. He felt slightly uneasy as the camera came to life. *Did I delete all the files?*

The first picture appeared showing a group of people. "These few might not interest you," he said moving through the pictures but allowing the man to see as he changed to the next frame. He finally stopped in one of the frames. "This is where he lived when he was a kid," he said. He turned to the following picture. "These are his initials. I found it on the sidewalk next to the apartment where he lived with his mother."

Gutierrez tried to look interested, but the look in his eyes showed otherwise. Timing it perfectly he looked at his watch. "I think you should get going Mr. Lopez."

"Oh," Lopez said turning to him. "Yeah, you're right." He noticed his bag being pushed toward him.

"Lt. Gutierrez," he said extending his hand. "A pleasure."

The man shook his hand. "Likewise."

"Gentlemen," Lopez said grabbing his bag and walking away not waiting for an answer.

Conner looked at his watch once again as he continued working on the report. His mind, however, was on the small picture on the side of his laptop.

He had linked his laptop to Dexter's main computer, something that wasn't necessary since Dexter was in the guesthouse outside. Conner did not want to wait the extra 10-15 seconds that would take Dexter to go back to the house. No, Conner wanted to know immediately when Flight 126 from Havana to Miami was airborne.

"Hey," the voice of Ann came from behind him.

He was about to turn when he felt her hands on his shoulders. For the first few days they had tried to avoid any type of contact in front of the other agents, something that they gave up trying after realizing that everyone was on to them. The situation, however, had changed drastically in the past few days. Ever since Becker returned, Conner had made multiple attempts to talk to her alone. That had not happened, until now.

"Relax, everything will be fine," she said softly.

He grabbed her hands and turned around, finally facing her.

"I'm sorry," he said looking into her eyes. "I didn't know what else to do. I needed information and—"

"Don't," she stopped him. "When you suggested it, I was more than apprehensive."

"I know."

"But, I have to admit, I'm glad I met with him."

"You are?"

"For the first time in my life, I realize that I should stop trying to avoid him. He is my father and everyone knows that. I have no reason to hide it, not anymore." Becker moved even closer to him. "As a matter of fact; I asked him to join me for dinner, once this is all over."

Conner smiled as she wrapped her arms around him. "What did he say?"

"He said yes, as long as I bring you along. He wants to meet you."

"Me? Really?"

"Oh yeah!" She moved around the chair and sat on him.

"So what exactly does that mean?" Conner asked.

"It means that you are in serious trouble mister."

Conner smiled and kissed her, not caring about the other agents in the house.

Chapter 24

===================

Michael Lopez felt exhausted from the restless night he had. He could not sleep knowing that he had information that could easily get him killed. Even at work, he found himself too tired to concentrate yet anxiously waiting for some kind of a signal.

He arrived from Cuba the previous afternoon and, as directed, went about his daily routine; not making any contact but waiting for someone to reach him. Conner told him that they needed to make sure he wasn't being watched.

Lopez arrived and went directly to his mother. He didn't visit her often, only on weekends and to check on her from time to time. After a shower and dinner, he sat and talked to her about all the family members that came to visit. His family in Cuba was all she had left, something that constantly worried her. This was good for her; talking about them; knowing that they were all well. It also helped him pass the time.

The office was not expecting him until two days later but the moment he arrived he knew he would return to work early; he needed the distraction.

Returning home, he went through his mail as his computer booted up. He wanted to do some work before returning to the office; he was mistaken.

After an hour, he turned off the computer frustrated. He could not concentrate; instead he found a hiding place for the disc and placed his laptop next to his bed.

"Hey Mike," the voice of a woman called from outside his office.

Lopez realized that he had dozed off once again. *I should've stayed home today,* he thought.

"Mike?" the voice said a little louder.

"Janet, what's up?"

"We got a call from the second floor; it seems that there's a glitch in the last section of codes you gave them. They were wondering if you could go down and check it for them."

"Sure," he said getting up from his chair. After retrieving the disc from his drawer he reached for the laptop and walked out of his office.

He was not sure if this was the call; he knew that the testers worked on the second floor but he had not given them any new data since last week. Even if they were really calling, he was not planning to leave the information alone in his office.

Tamargo was feeling more at ease.

He arrived in Havana with Conner's words still in his mind. Conner was apprehensive about sending him, worried that something would happen. True, he volunteered, but he knew that he was the only person of the group best suited for the job and at the time it seemed like a good idea to visit the island. When the plane touched down at Jose Marti airport, Tamargo had changed his mind.

The soldiers bothered him at first but it wasn't until he realized that he was alone that he began to fear for his life. This was not his first trip to a hostile area, but the previous time he knew he had back up. The last time he knew he wasn't alone, he knew that help was only a call away. Here, he was alone, about to meet a man that could be waiting for him with the Cuban Secret Service.

To his relief, Eduardo Peralta was waiting for him, alone.

Within hours Peralta took Tamargo on a tour of Havana, showing him some of the tourist attractions. "We must wait," Peralta said. "If they are watching us, they will get tire by tomorrow night."

At night, the two men sat in a bar, a statue of Ernest Hemingway stood in the corner of the bar, as if he was drinking and sharing stories with the patrons. Tamargo didn't know if Peralta was trying to get him drunk, trying to find more information on him. In fact, he did not care. He arrived in Havana knowing very little, something that Conner had insisted on.

"The less you know," Conner said. "The better it will be for you."

Between the drinks Tamargo came to the realization that ever since the beginning Conner was setting him up to visit the island. *I don't know anything!* He said to himself.

Peralta didn't ask him; instead the man began to slowly back down when Tamargo started to talk to one of the girls in a nearby table.

The Slovakian blonde he met the night before knew very little Spanish but apparently he must have said something right. As he woke up to his first morning in Havana, Tamargo felt her body move closer to his.

The trip to the second floor was a complete waste of time. As Lopez thought, the testers were done with the codes he sent them before leaving and were now busy working on a game that was ready for release.

Lopez pressed the button of the elevator ready to return to his office.

"Going up?" the man asked as the door opened almost immediately.

Lopez nodded and walked in, pressing his floor.

The elevator ascended, passing Lopez' floor without sign of stopping. Michael looked at the numbers and quickly looked back at the man riding the car with him.

"Conner wants to meet you, sir," the man said without looking at him.

The car stopped in the 8th floor and Lopez followed Hawkins down the empty corridor to an office listed as 'Dr. Calderon.' Lopez noticed that the door to the office was not locked as they both entered the patients' waiting area.

A buzzer sounded and the man opened the door and signal for Michael to enter.

"Third door on the right."

"Thanks," Lopez replied walking in.

"Michael!" Conner shouted. "How are you? Did you have a good trip?"

"Actually, yes!" Lopez replied.

"Did you get to visit the places you wanted to visit?"

"Yes, mostly thanks to you. Transportation there is horrible but the man had a decent car. I don't understand how people can survive like that for so long."

Conner nodded. "Considering what proud people they still are; it is amazing."

Lopez knew that although Conner was showing interest in his life; he was here for only one reason. He placed his bag on a table and began to unzip it.

"No Michael, follow me."

The two men went to an adjacent room were a man was sitting by a desk; his eyes fixed on the computer screen while his fingers raced through the keyboard.

"Michael, meet Richard Dexter," Conner said.

"Hello," Lopez said extending his hand.

The man failed to notice Lopez' hand, his eyes not moving from the screen. "Hey Mike. One more minute boss; I think I got it."

"Come on Dexter; he's already here."

Lopez took the opportunity to finish unzipping the bag. He removed the laptop from the bag and set it next to the bag. From the side pocket of his cargo pants he removed the disc and handed it to Conner.

Conner looked at the disc in amusement. "Save it; that's a blank copy."

Michael looked at the disc and back at Conner. He opened his mouth but decided not to say anything.

Conner's attention was again on the computer screen. "Dexter, give it a break."

"Okay, fine!" the man said pushing the chair back. He rose from the chair and patted on the backrest. "Have a seat Michael."

Michael moved around the table and sat on the chair; immediately shocked to see his game on Dexter's computer.

"Before we start I want to say that I'm a big fan," Dexter commented. "I love 'Black Iris'."

"Thanks," Michael said.

"Going back to this game, I know that the file is somewhere behind this door," Dexter said pointing at a large metal door in the game. "I also know that the only way to open the door is from level 23, which as you can see it's where we are."

Lopez was amazed, looking at the screen and back at the man hovering around him.

"Dexter is one of our best computer geeks." Conner said.

"I played this game almost a year ago," Dexter said. "It was pretty good; although I thought some of the bosses were a little too easy."

Lopez acted uninterested, his attention fully on the screen before him.

"Anyway," Dexter continued. "The file is somewhere in this room, and my best estimate is that it is behind the door."

Michael nodded.

"The problem is that every time I open the door the game goes into a cut-scene; followed by a boss that I can't seem to beat. This boss was never that hard but now I can't seem to kill him."

Lopez smiled; he had stumped one of the CIA's computer experts.

"It's simple," he said moving his game character toward the door. As the door began to open Lopez pressed a few keys. Dexter tried to follow but could not figure out which keys the man typed.

The cut scene played again; Dexter noticed that nothing had changed from the countless times he tried it in the past.

The game return to playing mode as a large man with a battle-axe rushed to Lopez' character. Lopez pressed a key and his soldier put the shotgun he was holding on the floor. Pressing another key, Lopez made his character crouch.

The battle-axe came down and hit the Lopez' character directly on the head.

"What are you doing?" Dexter asked looking at the health bar diminishing.

"You are dead!" The computer boss spitted delivering another atrocious hit. The health bar changed from yellow to red.

Michael watched carefully as the computer boss lifted the axe once again.

"You see Richard," he said placing his fingers on the keyboard. "Your instinct is always to fight back."

The axe began to come down and Lopez pressed a few keystrokes. Dexter wasn't sure if he had pressed the same keys or not. Whatever he had done, the axe was now stopped in mid-strike.

Lopez began to type rapidly; Dexter no longer looking at the keyboard, watched the screen in front of them.

As Lopez continued to type, the game began to fade into darkness, returning the player once again, to the front of the door.

"Impressive!" Dexter said.

"It's not done yet." Lopez pressed the key for opening the door and a keypad appeared. After typing a string of numbers a message appeared. ***"Access granted!"***

The door opened up to a black screen with a small icon in the middle.

"There you go!" Lopez smiled back at Dexter as he rose from the chair.

"Wow!" Dexter replied pressing the file from his current position. "No wonder NSA asked for your help."

Conner extended his hand and Lopez took it. "Thanks!"

"Is there anything we can do for Navarro?" Lopez asked.

"Soon enough," Conner said. "Right now we need to take care of whatever is going on."

Lopez noticed Conner looking at his laptop. "You want me to erase the file from my laptop?"

Conner smiled reaching for his pocket, "It's already taken care of."

"Somehow, I'm not surprised."

"Here," Conner said handing him an envelope. "Trip to Hawaii for two and a little something for your bank account." Conner noticed the look in Lopez' face. "Our way of saying, thank you."

Chapter 25

====================

They were waiting for him at the table; everyone dressed in business casual. Conner smiled as he stood by the head of the table. To his right, Becker was sitting already studying the files she had passed to the other two members. Hawkins sat across from her, the folder still closed as he waited for the order to open the documents. The chair next to Hawkins was still empty as Dexter continued working in the kitchen.

"Almost done boss," he shouted. "Start without me."

"Very well," Conner said. "Before we begin, I just want to say that I had a long talk with Kyle Clark at NSA, it seems that they found their leak. Apparently one of the assistants was selling satellite information to the Cubans. At the moment we are using that to our advantage. We will continue to allow this information to 'leak'."

Dexter returned from the kitchen with a full plate of food.

Conner ignored him and continued. "Mr. Clark's team will be checking the feeds for anything unusual. In addition, we received good intel from our man in Cuba.

Although it was a one shot deal, our man delivered tremendously."

Ann Becker noticed herself nodding in agreement.

"We know that the base at Lourdes is having 'technical' difficulties. As you know Lourdes is more than a military base. This base, and a second one in Bejucal, has been somewhat of an annoyance to us in the past few years. The amounts of communication and listening devices in those two bases have been a constant problem, until now. Apparently the lack of Soviet support has rendered some of the microwave towers, in Lourdes, useless. We've also been assured that the radar installation in Bejucal has been considerably reduced in power due to lack of parts."

Conner noticed everyone looking at the report as he continued. "Sources indicate that the Cuban government is demanding parts from Russia but so far there is no official answer. We persuaded the Russians to delay any supplies for at least a month."

Conner untwisted the cap from a bottle of water but decided against drinking.

"Regardless of the status of these two places; we should continue to treat it as if they were at 100%."

He took a drink from the bottle and put it down. "Questions?" He waited for any, "Good, let's continue."

There was a noise from one of the chairs as Dexter tried to get comfortable.

"Our man also is warning us of two future movements in the Cuban military."

As he spoke, everyone turned to the next page.

"First, it appears that our fears were correct. The Cuban army is planning some kind of move southeast. The plan is for tanks and supply trucks to be moved to Santiago de Cuba. So Gitmo is definitely a target."

Becker agreed. "Guantanamo has been a thorn to Castro ever since he came to power. He would love to see that base destroyed."

Conner continued. "Also, and this is important. The original plan for this movement was to start on June 23rd. The date was changed to early July. Our man in Cuba could not explain the change in schedule."

"You think Tamargo's visit affected their schedule?" Becker asked.

"I think so," Conner replied.

"I have a question," Hawkins said raising his hand. "Why would he attack Gitmo? I mean I know that he hates us but the base has been in the island through his entire regime."

"To be honest Hawkins, I don't know." Conner replied. "People might say that he's a madman in some path of revenge against us for doing who knows what to him. In truth, I think he is a very calculating man, taking advantage of the situation as he sees it. A crazy madman would not have survived all those years." Conner sipped more water before he continued. "I do think that he is losing power, somehow Marcano's influence got to him. I think for the first time in his life he feels vulnerable."

"But why attack our base?" Hawkins asked.

"Maybe because he believes that he has superior firepower in comparison to the base. Maybe because he doesn't want his revolution to end like the Soviet Union, or maybe he just wants to die fighting."

Hawkins scribbled something and returned the pencil to the table, perfectly aligned with the papers. "Thank you, sir."

Conner nodded and continued. "The second movement concerns the Cuban Air Force. Our contact indicates that there are plans to move all newer fighter and bombers to bases in the northern section of the province of Havana. The only other base mentioned, outside Havana, is in Varadero, also in the northern part of the island."

Once again Hawkins raised his hand.

Conner pointed at him, realizing that the large man was slowly becoming more communicative.

"Given your previous assumption, we could also assume that the planned move of fighters and bombers could be to attack a target in our coast."

Conner nodded.

"But, most of the fighters have enough range to reach Miami from anywhere in the island. Why move them?"

"Assuming that this is the reason," Conner said. "A large wave moving from their closest location might hit us by surprise. It would be easier to coordinate and give them more fuel to return to different bases throughout the island."

Again Hawkins wrote something down.

"I don't have to tell any of you why Miami would be the target." Conner said looking at Hawkins.

The man remained silent.

"Largest population of Cubans," Becker interrupted. "The amount of successful Cuban businesses and corporations; you could add to that all the different anti-Castro organizations and entities."

Conner turned his attention back to the papers.

"Our contact provided us with name of some of the bases, as well as maps. He also provided us with some of the names of the people in charge of the operations. Two of the names are causing a commotion in Langley. Colonel Antonio Guerra has been promoted to General. At this point, the whereabouts of General Guerra are unknown.

The second man is Colonel Fernando Chavez. Three years ago the man was plotting an attack on the Naval Base at Guantanamo. Chavez was removed from his command and was moved to a base in Pinar Del Rio.

According to this paper, Chavez will be in charge of all tank divisions moving to the southeast."

He looked around waiting for questions, there were none.

"Hopefully we might be able to get more information once we get the new satellite feeds from Clark. This will probably not happen until Tamargo returns."

"What about the dates?" Becker asked. "At first there seemed to be significance on the dates however things have died down."

"We are still investigating the attacks in South America on June 14. As you all know by our dates, June 14 is the birthday of Ernesto 'Che' Guevara. On June 14th there were multiple blasts in cities in both Bolivia and Argentina. The attacks could have been coincidence, or some kind of movement trying to make a statement. As I said, it is still being investigated.

As of right now we have one more date: July 12th. This date is a minor day in the history of the revolution so I believe we might see something happening but nothing large enough to attract attention. The next one however, is one of the biggest dates in Castro's Cuba: July 26th. This was the name of their movement, this was what they called themselves, nothing is more important to the revolution than July 26th.

We do have to realize that the original date, what started it all was a futile attack by a small group of rebels on a large barrack. I think that says a lot."

There was a silence around the table.

"Our top priority right now is to find any Soviet made SS-22 missiles. These missiles have a range of over 200 kilometers and a newer specification has them at a cruise speed of Mach 2.3."

"SS-22, I've seen that before?" Hawkins asked.

Conner looked at the man. "You've seen something on these missiles.

He moved through some of the papers he was carrying in another folder, his eyes quickly scanning through the reports. "Here it is. According to a Cuban deserter back in the late 90's, the Cubans were experimenting with biological weapons delivered in SS-22's. The claims were believed to be a hoax since there was no evidence of any SS-22 missiles in Cuba."

"They have the missiles," Conner said.

Dexter's voice was serious. "Clark and I are working on it. Wherever they are, they're keeping it very well hidden but we'll find them."

"Good, keep me posted."

"Hawkins, how are things going with Murray?"

Hawkins sat up straight; something Conner thought would be impossible. "There are six people we are following very closely. She's monitoring their moves, as well as any calls they make."

"Please make sure they are not picked up until we say so."

"She knows, sir."

"Good."

Conner addressed everyone once again. "In the meantime, please review your files and I want you to come up with anything, no matter how stupid you think it might be."

He turned to Becker; "I need to see you right now so please stay." He did not have to say anything else, almost immediately both Dexter and Hawkins began to leave.

"I called my father," she said as the man cleared the room. "He has no more information."

"Thank you," he replied. "That's not why I asked you to stay."

She raised her head, her eyes looking into his.

"I talked to Van Buren, Novloskov's findings were correct the Cubans have the warheads and the means to deliver them.

"The SS missiles? Becker asked.

"We need to find them," Conner said.

Antonio Tamargo did not think of himself as a risk taker, and yet he still wondered what the CIA saw in him. He saw himself as a shy, mild-manner, person who liked everything in a certain order. Even after months working for the agency, Tamargo could not understand what made them choose him above all other candidates. And yet, here he was.

He shocked himself when he volunteered on this mission, thinking that Conner would ignore his request with some excuse about his lack of experience. At first Tamargo thought that he was exactly what Conner was looking for, a young inexperienced agent with no information. He had neither the information nor the expertise to be a great loss.

He truly wasn't a risk taker, but now he sat on the couch watching as Eduardo Peralta tried unsuccessful to get up from his chair.

"What did you do to me?" Peralta asked reaching for his phone.

Tamargo held the phone tightly in his hand trying hard to ignore the trembling. Tomorrow he would be back in the states, giving Conner a report that Tamargo knew was a lie. Eduardo Peralta had done an amazing job in showing him everything he came to the island for; it was exactly what he hoped for. Something bothered Tamargo since the beginning. It was not the information that Peralta provided, or the ease in which they were able to move about the island.

Peralta was more than the perfect host, except for the first night when he tried unsuccessfully to get information from him. Tamargo was immune to alcohol, as well as some drugs, something that Conner probably knew since it was on his file.

At the time Tamargo played the part, answering all the questions that Peralta asked him, it was easy, since he truly did not know anything. He wasn't supposed to try anything, his orders were simple: gather the information that Peralta provided and return home. That was until he arrived.

He did not remember why he brought the drugs, but almost immediately he knew he would use them.

"Now," he said finally. "I want to know what's really going on."

He listened as Peralta began to talk, knowing well that the man will not remember anything afterwards.

Chapter 26

==================

"It's time," Conner said looking at his watch one more time. He could not believe how fast a week passed. At this time the plane that would be taking Tamargo back to Miami would be taking off from Jose Marti Airport.

"We could drive him to the FBI building," Henderson said. "Make it look like we're part of the case as well."

"No! I want him to be whisked away as soon as possible. We're supposed to be desperate."

"I agree," Becker said walking between the two men.

"So we'll do it as you asked," Henderson said. "Aguila and I will be waiting for him by the tarmac door. We'll exit through those stairs, making it look official. I will personally drive him to the waiting plane."

"Good," Conner said. "Advice Tamargo that this is per Van Buren's instructions, he'll understand."

"Got it!" Henderson said. "I'll call you after the plane is in the air."

"Thanks!" Conner said shaking the man's hand.

Henderson said good-bye to Becker and drove away."

"Little drastic, isn't it?" Becker said.

"Moving Tamargo like that? Actually, it was my idea." Conner said. "We don't know what type of influence Tamargo received in the island. He might be a liability now."

Becker raised an eyebrow.

"I discussed it with Van Buren." Conner said in protest.

She smiled at him. "It's not that, it's just that you're really fitting into the boss' role all too well."

Conner remained speechless as she turned and walked back into the house.

The phone rang a third time before Eduardo Peralta pressed the speaker button.

"Oigo?" Peralta answered.

"Hola Eduardo, es Pedro." The voice said nervously.

"Pedro, how are things in Miami?"

"That's the reason why I called you. Our friend arrived at 3:00 O'clock this afternoon."

"Yes, I'm aware of that." Peralta's eyes shifted to the man walking around the desk and standing next to his chair.

Domingo Maldonado could've heard the conversation as well from where he was sitting only a minute before. Even though this was not his office he hated to sit on the opposite side of the desk.

"It seems that they are taking this very serious. Our friend never made it to the terminal."

"Oh? What do you mean?"

"According to my contact, he was moved to a private jet, which took off 5 minutes later."

"Any idea on—"

"They also told me that a very high CIA official was in that plane."

Peralta noticed the smile in Maldonado's face.

"Very well Pedro. I think this is exactly what we were hoping for."

"Is there anything else?"

"Not for now. I'll call you if I need any further assistance."

"Well, goodbye then." Davila said.

There was no answer as Peralta had severed the connection.

"What do you think Eduardo?" Maldonado said from behind him.

"Sir, I believe that we were the only contact they could find."

"Yes, it appears so." Maldonado walked to the window and looked outward. A view of the bay could be seen in the distance.

"They also find it extremely important if they moved him away so quickly."

"True, yet they are still treating it as a minor problem; otherwise they would've had a team already in Miami."

"Sir, do you think they bought the whole Venezuela connection?"

"What do you mean?" Maldonado asked moving back from the window.

"I don't know. How could be concentrating so much in helping another country when we were just attacked?"

"You're right, in a way Eduardo." Maldonado returned and sat back on the chair. "We have punished who we believed committed this crime against our patria. We will continue to blame the Yankees but we should also look into the future. Venezuela is on the brink of a civil war and we will support the current government with our military might. In turn, he will help us with our current energy crisis."

Peralta realized that it was a good argument.

"Look Eduardo, the man had no clue what was happening in the rest of the island. You whisked him to Pinar Del Rio almost immediately and what he saw was more than enough proof that you were being honest."

"And the two Venezuelan military cargo planes helped," Peralta said with a smile.

"We'll see what happens in the next couple of days."

Chapter 27

=================

Tamargo returned with a large amount of information; detailed plans that seemed completely legitimate.

According to the papers given to him by Peralta, Havana was preparing to move troops and equipment to Venezuela. The current situation in that country was becoming unstable and Castro promised to help eliminate the opposition, which now was building momentum.

The type of equipment and locations that Tamargo photographed and described agreed with the satellite feeds they continued to receive. That troubled Conner.

Could I be wrong? He continued to ask himself.

"No!" he said firmly. The satellites agree with Tamargo's story but only for now.

Although the 'scheduled' pass showed no activity, the new bird was showing something different. The troops were not concentrating on the main two airports on the island. Instead, there seemed to be a slow movement to the southeast. It was not noticeable yet but Conner knew that it would soon change.

The second set of notes, sent to him in the same package made him realized how right he was about Tamargo. The notes were half-written words done by what Conner could only surmise as a very shaky hand. On the side, a small note was written on a yellow 'post-it' note, place perfectly against the bottom right corner of the paper. *You were right about the kid, he's got balls. –V.B.*

Conner removed the 'post-it' notes and read the notes more carefully this time. The ringing on the phone startled him.

"Conner," he said answering it.

"Steven, it's Van Buren."

"Yes sir," Conner shifted on his chair.

"Did you read the 'Times'?" Van Buren asked.

"No sir."

"The headlines read, 'US protest Cuban involvement in Venezuela'. I'm afraid someone leaked the information. We are beginning an investigation immediately. I'm sure it'll be on the papers soon."

"That's a shame sir." Conner tried not to smile at Van Buren's sarcasm. He knew that the leak was Van Buren's way to escalate the Venezuela story. "Hope this thing doesn't get blown out of proportion."

"I'll worry about that. Did you get the notes?"

"Yes sir."

"It seemed you were right about him, as well as your hunches."

Conner remained silent.

"The information we got from your two sources got everyone's attention. There are meetings going on right now all over town." Van Buren paused slightly. Conner realized the old man was probably enjoying his morning coffee.

Without warning, Van Buren continued. "Did you find your man yet?"

"Yes sir; his team is already assembled and currently in Homestead."

"Perfect. There's going to be a lot of activities in the next few days, including a couple of incidents. I need you to remain focused."

"Yes sir."

"We're going to have a really rough time for the next month, Steven."

"As long as we're prepared sir; I'll handle the rough time."

"I want you and Becker to remain ghosts. I'll handle the politics."

"Yes sir."

"Tamargo will remain here; I think you have enough people down there already."

"I agree sir."

"Good man. I will call you as soon as I have more for you."

"Thank you sir."

Conner hung up the phone noticing Becker standing by the door.

"Did you see the paper today?" Becker asked.

"The Venezuela thing? We were just talking about it." Conner pulled a chair and she sat next to him. "Van Buren says that we should remain as ghosts."

"That's highly irregular." Becker complained.

"This whole thing about Venezuela is going to get worse. There will be investigations and maybe a hearing. Van Buren feels that it will be the best way to keep us under the radar."

Becker had no comment.

"This also means that we're directly reporting to him, at least until this thing is over. Nobody knows what we are working on."

"So what's our next move?"

"We are to remain on stand-by until he calls. He will have more information then."

"What do you think?" she asked seriously.

"We've done what we can. Now, we need to wait."

Raul Castro looked once again inside the dark room and closed the door behind him. Maldonado, sitting on Fidel Castro's desk watched as Raul returned to the office.

"How is he doing?" Maldonado asked.

"Not good," Raul Castro said. "The doctor was here just a few hours ago; he had to increase the dosage. I don't know how he manages with the amount of drug in his system."

"He is a strong man, stronger than most I've met."

Castro nodded. "He spend almost three days without a single shot, I don't know how he could control the pain."

Maldonado shook his head. "What's the prognosis?"

"His muscles are deteriorating at a more rapid speed than we anticipated. He feels that by the end of the year, he will probably be paralyzed. His mind however, will be as sharp as ever."

Again Maldonado shook his head. "Hard to see a man of action like him deteriorating to such a state."

"Yes," Castro said. "Given the choice, I would rather die fighting as well."

Fidel Castro's eyes were closed, the pain on his body only a dull sensation now. He fought the doctor's order to take the shot; he did not want his mind being affected by any type of painkillers.

Unfortunately the pain was becoming unbearable and he needed to rest.

The dosage was larger than before, enough to make the pain subside, enough to make a normal man fall asleep almost immediately; but not him. He remained quiet, listening to his brother and Maldonado talk. He felt anger at the way they were discussing his health like an old pathetic man that was dying. He felt even angrier at his muscles, as they continue to deteriorate making him feel weak.

Yes, Raul was right. He would prefer to die fighting than continue living in this state. He did not want to see people looking at him in pity. He did not want his enemy to see a sign of weakness in him. No, Fidel Castro will die as he lived all his life, fighting.

Unlike others, he knew the exact day he would die, July 26. It was exactly how he planned it, exactly how he wanted it. A day in which all Cubans will mourn and celebrate, be it those who love him or those who hate him.

Patria o Muerte, he thought. For it was his country, his island, his revolution or it was death. He smiled knowing that the day would soon be near.

Chapter 28

===================

Captain Angel Acosta felt his teeth grinding as the rattling continue all around him.

"This plane is a death trap," he said to himself holding the joystick even tighter.

The Russian-made Mikoyan-Gurevich 21 sluggishly complied to Acosta's command as it left Cuban waters.

Acosta volunteered for this mission, one that could place him in harms way. The task was simple: fly the old MiG-21 Fishbed north until intercepted by American fighters. He was not to engage, but rather ask for political asylum. His mission, like others before him, was to test the American readiness in case of an attack.

Unfortunately, nobody told him he would be flying the worse shaped fighter in the entire Cuban Air Force.

Acosta looked at the speed in disgust as the plane continued to tremble around him.

"Ten miles to land, do these people even know I'm here?" Acosta wondered as the Fishbed continued to struggle to maintain its cruising speed of 950 km/h.

"Sir, the two F-15's are approaching the south marker, Captain Lewis is requesting to intercept."

Admiral James McKnight ignored the voice calling from behind. He knew Captain Lewis was given an order and although he would question the reason, he would not intercept the MiG unless instructed. Lewis, however, was right.

"Lieutenant, advise Captain Lewis to return to base. Also advice Homestead Air Reserve that we appreciate all the help provide it."

"Yes sir."

McKnight turned to the other officer who immediately began to relay information to the two F-18 Hornets sitting on the runway on the Key West Naval Air Station. The glass around the tower vibrated slightly as the afterburners of the two F-18s took the fighters into the air. McKnight picked up a headset and immediately put it on. Pressing the button he connected to the Hornet's leader.

"Cassidy, this is McKnight."

"Sir!" the voice in the com-link responded.

"Target is six miles and closing. I want him intercepted at exactly two miles from land, not before."

"Yes sir," Lieutenant Cassidy replied.

"Johnny," the Admiral said. "Impress our guest."

"Understood sir."

Admiral McKnight took off the headset and walked to one of the nearby windows. "It started," he said.

"Close to two miles," Acosta said, his eyes scanning the sky for anything. The radar had shown two blips but they faded almost immediately. "So much for protecting their borders."

The fighters came fast and they came close. Acosta noticed only the blur, and at the time he was unable to distinguish what type of planes they were. Instead, he felt his plane rattle even stronger as the turbulences left by the fighters attacked his plane.

Acosta jerked in his seat, his head looking around for the two fighters as his hands continued to hold the stick, trying to make the Fishbed steady itself.

The two F-18s eased on each side on his plane; slowly closing the gap between them. Acosta kept the plane level, his eyes fixed at the pilot on his right side, who he could see clearly now.

The pilot did not seem upset, instead he signaled for Acosta to start descending. Acosta turned to the other pilot who was signaling in the same manner. Acosta gave the two pilots the 'thumbs up' signal as he continued to keep the plane level between the two Hornets. He had studied these planes in the past, learning its capabilities, its weakness. Acosta was not impressed by the F-18, which he considered no match for his personal favorite, the MiG-29.

Once again he looked at the first fighter, his face smiling at the pilot while his eyes scanned the plane. Immediately, he turned to the other fighter with the same intentions.

In contrast to the two Air-to-Air missiles under his wings, the Hornets were unarmed. For a moment Acosta wished he were meeting them under different circumstance. Even piloting the Fishbed, Acosta believed he could destroy both planes.

The three planes began to descend as the naval base's runway became visible. Acosta noticed the two Hornets beginning to fall behind giving him room to maneuver.

"Here we go!" he said lowering his landing gear.

Chapter 29

=================

It had been an exhausting week and Conner realized that it was only the beginning. Shortly after speaking to Van Buren the phone calls began. At first, Conner was amused as the questions and scenarios being considered, but the amusement was short-lived. The calls from high-ranking Admirals and Generals continued, as each demanded more and more time from Conner.

He had scheduled appointments with the commanders of the Homestead Air Reserve Base, Key West Naval Air Base, and even the Naval Base in Guantanamo, Cuba. Most important was his meeting tomorrow, which will include the National Security Advisor and members of the Intelligent Section for the Air Force and Navy.

The events that began at mid-afternoon however, changed the plans for the days. As the plane carrying him taxied near a hangar at the naval base in Key West, Conner could see the activity around the recently arrived Russian made fighter.

Stepping off the plane he was greeted by the Navy liaison officer waiting for him.

"Who's doing the interrogation?" Conner asked the man as they walked away from the plane.

"Lt. Martinez," the liaison replied. "He was stationed at Gitmo during the time we were detaining all the Cubans. He got some valuable information then."

The two men walked into a small building near the hangar where the MiG was being thoroughly checked.

"Would you believe those Air-to-Air missiles are dummies?" the liaison officer said.

Conner looked back at the plane as the man opened the door.

"Kind of old, isn't it?" Conner asked.

"Yes sir."

The room Conner entered was small, made crowded by an array of video and recording equipment. In front, a large window showed the Cuban pilot sitting at a table as Lt. Martinez continued his questioning.

"Two way mirror?" Conner asked.

"Not quite. From the other side it looks like wood panel; makes it easier for them." The officer looked through one of the vidcams and turned back to Conner. "We got it after that MiG pilot gave us that scare back in 97."

Conner continued to watch the two men talking.

"What do you have so far?"

"He's a very friendly guy, really talkative; doesn't seem nervous at all."

Conner said nothing.

"He claims that their air force is in shambles; most of their planes are grounded or barely flying. He was the one that commented on the missiles, said they are done to show their might."

"You think he's serious?"

"I don't know sir. "He also mentioned that the Russians took most of the MiG-29s because Cuba did not pay for them."

Conner was now amused. "He seriously thinks we are going to believe that?"

"He said that there were a few in his base but that they were removed within the last six months. Claims he hasn't seen a MiG 29 or even a 25 since January of this year."

"What else?"

"Martinez asked about troop movements."

"Troop movement?" Conner asked alarmed.

"We wanted to know more information on that Venezuela connection that's been in the news."

"Right," Conner said. "Did he have any information on that?"

"He said he wasn't really aware of anything except for army personnel getting ready to be deployed to Venezuela."

The two men noticed Martinez opening the door and waited as the Navy officer walked into their room.

"He's really good; but he's lying." Martinez said.

"I agree, but we are going to give him the benefit of the doubt." Conner added. "Has he eaten?"

"Yes, and he ate like he hadn't in days. The only thing that he has been asking for is to make a phone call to a relative here in Florida."

"Any idea who this person is?"

"He hasn't given me any names, but I could ask him."

"No!" Conner said. "Give him access to a phone, but not in that room. I want him to feel a little more comfortable. Move him to someone's office, but make sure we get a trace and a recording of that call."

"Yes sir." Martinez excused himself and headed for the offices nearby. A few minutes later he returned to escort the pilot to a telephone.

Captain Acosta was slightly confused. He was expecting a more formal interrogation, conducted by either an intelligence agent or FBI. Instead a navy officer was asking him all the questions. An officer who seemed more concerned for his well being than for the information he could provide. Even more confusing was the fact that he was being shown to a regular telephone so that he could call his relative in Fort Lauderdale.

He was told that the interrogation would be long and arduous. They told him that they would be watching his every move. In truth, he was wondering if the information they gave him was more propaganda than the truth. He was no spy, only a soldier doing his job. Perhaps the Americans really believed that he was tire of living under the regime any longer.

He picked up the phone waiting for some kind of noise; any kind of sign that he was being recorded; he heard none.

"Do you have his number?" Martinez asked.

"Si," Acosta said pulling a piece of paper.

"Area code is 954," Martinez said. "That's the area code for Fort Lauderdale."

Acosta pretended to be confused but understood what Martinez was saying.

"You first need to dial 99 to get a line outside the base."

Acosta did as he was told.

"You then dial 1 for long distance and the number."

Again Acosta complied.

"Now is my turn." Martinez dialed a number noticing the look in Acosta's face. "That is my identification number. It is required for long distance call from the base."

"Oh, si; entiendo." Acosta said.

Martinez moved away enough for Acosta to have a private conversation. He knew every word was being recorded, he also needed to copy the number before he would forget."

"It's ringing," the lieutenant said as the two men stood behind him.

"Would he be bold enough to pass a message across?" the liaison officer asked.

"Bold? I'm more than willing to bet that he is bold enough." Conner added.

Conner listened as the pilot spoke in Spanish to the man who answered the phone. Although Conner was able to understand the language, it was impossible for him to keep up with the rapid way the two men were speaking.

In less than two minutes the conversation was over.

"Call's over," the ensign announced turning off the recorder. He pressed the 'eject' button on the machine and handed the disc to Conner.

"Good job, Conner said to the lieutenant.

"Thank you sir," the kid answered back.

"Anything else you need, sir?" the liaison officer asked him as he opened the door for Conner.

"I'm going to need a copy of the interrogation." Conner said walking out.

"You'll have it by your plane before you leave sir. Both paper and disc."

"Thanks," Conner said.

The men continued walking through the hangar, the MiG sitting inside as men continued to comb through it.

"What's going to happen to the pilot?"

"We know less about the pilot than we know about the plane. The Cubans are already asking for the plane and we want to give it to them as soon as possible, for obvious reasons. We have two more squadrons coming from Jacksonville as soon as that plane gets out."

Conner looked back at the old MiG sitting in the hangar.

"As for the pilot?" the liaison officer continued. "We have no idea right now."

The man showed him to a door and stood by the side. "Admiral McKnight is waiting for you."

"Thank you," Conner said opening the door.

Chapter 30

================

The Gulfstream G550 streaked through the sky at a cruising speed of Mach 0.80. Inside, Steve Conner felt as if the plane was standing still. Next to him Becker slept comfortably, something that Conner could not do. Although he felt exhausted by the trips, meetings, and phone calls, his mind continued to go over all the different places he had already visited.

The logistics in Key West weren't that complicated. Admiral McKnight had been briefed by the time Conner arrived and he had immediately prepared the base. Even before meeting Conner, McKnight was prepared. It was his decision to allow the MiG to come close before intercepting it. He was a good strategist and Conner figured that the base would be ready as he said. The only request McKnight made was immediately granted. Two squadrons of F-18 Hornets and one of F-14 Tomcats were schedule to arrive by July 15.

Like Key West, Homestead was preparing to receive multiple squadrons of fighters. Two squadrons of F-15s were scheduled to arrive on the 11th, followed by two squadrons of F-16s on the 14th. In addition, Homestead was also preparing to receive two battalions from the 1st Armored Division. Homestead would be ready, Conner was sure of this as well.

His biggest worry was still Gitmo. There were too many questions remaining, too many variables, and that was one thing that bothered Conner. It bothered him so much that he could not help but interrupt a discussion between the Secretary of Defense and the National Security Advisor. Conner could not figure why they were so worried about press releases and future elections when the only concern was to protect the base.

Van Buren said nothing, letting Conner realize that politicians have their priorities, not unlike them. It was later that he approached him. "Look Conner, I know you feel bad about the meeting but it wasn't your fault. You have to realize that they have their agendas and you have to let them talk things out before you bring the actual problems to the table. Of course, bringing September 11 to the picture surely accelerated things."

Conner felt embarrassed, but Van Buren's next comment changed that very quickly.

"Don't worry; you'll do better next time."

Next time? Conner thought

"Trust me son, they'll be a next time." Conner felt the director's heavy hand on his shoulder. "I have a strong feeling about it."

Of course, before the next time Conner had to prove himself in solving the problem he so eloquent brought to the table. Tomorrow he would have to figure out how to defend Guantanamo?

The phone woke Conner up; at least he thought he was asleep.

"Yes?" he said noticing Becker moving. "Great!"

Becker's eyes opened up as she noticed the look on Conner's face. The man's eyes looked tire but now they had a certain spark in them.

Conner pressed the 'off' button on the phone and turned to Becker. "We found the missiles."

"We have complications!" Raul Castro shouted as he walked into the room.

Fidel Castro said nothing, his body not even turning to see his brother.

"I just received information that an American carrier arrived at Guantanamo."

Fidel's eyes were closed and for a moment Raul thought the man was asleep.

"The USS Enterprise arrived a few hours ago." Fidel finally said. "I am aware of it. I have also sent a formal complaint stating that the carrier is a slap in the face to our country."

Raul said nothing, finally sitting next to his brother.

"We're also checking on the report that it is due to a new campaign the Americans are beginning in the Middle East. According to the latest report; they expect between 100-300 new prisoners in Guantanamo."

"I guess you are informed," Raul said.

"The carrier arrived with heavy lifters to aid on the supply ships."

"Supplies?" Raul asked.

"I know; it was extremely irregular to us as well; but two of our patrols confirmed that both ships were loaded with large crates labeled…" Fidel thought for a moment. "Oh yes, 'pre-fab. It seems they're bringing prefabricated houses. We were already advised that there would also be some heavy construction since there is no room for the new prisoners. This means that the base is going to be very busy for the next few months."

Raul tried to hide a smile.

"You see my brother; we have it all under control." Fidel finally moved, turning toward his brother. "Now, what do you have for me?"

Raul began almost immediately. "Our forces are beginning to move; we expect to be at 100% strength in another week. There were some problems with a few of the supply trucks but they are back on track. Unfortunately the only thing we are lacking is the extra supply of fuel we were promised."

"And you'll get it. A Venezuelan oil tanker will arrive tomorrow; everyone is aware of our need and it is our first priority, even ahead of the air force; which reminds me, where in hell is Contreras?"

"He was detained in Bejucal once again." Raul said. "He called to let me know that the power is down on the entire base."

Fidel ignored the comment. He was well aware of the situation and had given up on the base; concentrating on the plans ahead. He heard the footsteps behind him and immediately turned.

"Ah, Maldonado, what of our deserter?"

"Lieutenant Acosta landed safely in Cayo Hueso. He was allowed a phone call about five hours after he landed."

"Only five hours?" Raul asked

"My brother, why are you so edgy about every move the Americans make? They are too concern with the Middle East to be worrying about this small little island." Fidel waved for Maldonado to continue

"Acosta was intercepted only two miles from Cayo Hueso by two F-18 fighter planes. According to Acosta, the two planes had no visible weapons."

"Two miles?" Fidel said picking up a copy of the Miami Herald. He turned a few pages and turned to the article. "According the Herald, 'The Cuban plane was escorted by four fully armed fighters to the Naval Base. The fighters intercepted the Russian made MiG fighter more than 9 miles from US airspace." He was enjoying himself reading the article. "According to a military spokesman, we were never under any type of danger."

"Won't this make them more alert next time?" Maldonado asked

"Not necessarily," Raul interrupted. "We've seen this in the past; they will be wary for a few days but they will return to the normal procedure in little over a week."

Maldonado was about to continue when he noticed Fidel raising a finger. "What about our other plan?"

"General Guerra is already in charge of the situation." Raul replied. "Guerra has them hidden very well and they are nowhere near any installation for an American satellite to find them."

"Good," Fidel said.

"Good job guys; debriefing in ten minutes." Kristopher James said signaling for Conner to approach.

The group began to dissipate as Conner move closer.

"You know this PJ's are pretty good," James said.

"I thought the Air Force Para-Jumpers' were more involved with rescue and protection."

"Exactly! They have been excellent at protecting the 'facility'. They even gave us a major headache two days ago. I tell you I wouldn't mind having any of those guys in my team."

"Conner watched the men walk away.

"What's in the envelope?" James asked.

"A little present." Conner said handing him the package.

"Finally, something to work with."

"Sorry for the delay."

James tapped his fingers on the envelope."

"Let's walk," Conner said.

The two men walked away from the building; Conner looking behind his back a few times.

"Look Conner, I know things are escalating at a rapid pace. I've seen the activity in this base; something is happening soon. So, what's really going on; or are you going to keep this one away from me again?"

"I need you ready by the 15th, no later."

"We'll be ready." James said annoyed. "Hell, we're ready now."

"I came here to tell you; I owe you that much. I owe Reuben that."

"It's our job; it's what we sign up to do. Reuben was well aware of—"

"Would you shut up for one minute?"

James raised an eyebrow; his teeth clenched tightly.

"There has been some activity coming out of Cuba since the beginning of the year."

"I know that, I watch the news."

"No, I mean things that have gone unnoticed; things we have been collecting and made us come to a frightful conclusion."

"What's that?"

"Castro is planning a surprise attack on our country."

"You're joking!" James said almost bursting into a laugh.

"I'm dead serious. There has been large mobilization of troops and equipment."

"I thought that was part of their Venezuela campaign."

"Venezuela is a bluff; something to keep us looking in another direction. Something to make those moves seem normal."

"So what's the point of us going in?"

"Castro is planning an attack on both Gitmo and Miami; that we are certain of. That's why you are seeing so much activity here."

"Nothing to do with the Middle East?"

Conner shook his head. "We think we know when the attack is going to happen."

James's look intensified. "So what is it that you want from us? It seems that you have all the intel you need."

"Actually, there's something else."

"What?"

"Inside that envelope you have the plans to an old abandoned SAM site in Santa Clara. The place has been abandoned for years but there is activity now.

"Why the big interest in Surface-to-Air Missiles? What are you—" James stopped in mid-sentence. "There's something else isn't there?"

"Yes," Conner said.

The two men continued walking, stretching the distance between them and the base.

"Our interest is in the two trucks you'll see by the actual bunker. We have been searching for those missiles for weeks."

"I'm assuming you are not worried about a couple of planes being shot down," James said.

"No, we're more afraid at a whole city in the southeastern part of the US being erased."

"Wait, you mean to tell me…" James began.

"I'm not saying anything. I need you to secure the site and the missiles at any cost."

"James grinded his teeth. "Any cost?"

Conner said nothing.

"When do we leave?"

"Be ready on the 15th. We'll be monitoring the situation and mobilize you as soon as we have a window."

James stopped, making Conner stop a few feet ahead.

"You said you know when this attack is going to happen."

Conner nodded. "July 26th."

Chapter 31

===================

The parking lot at Homestead Air Reserve Base was still crowded as reporters continued to take one last shot of the group of armed servicemen leaving for the Middle East. The base was serving as a staging area giving the soldiers of the 1st Armored Division one last weekend of freedom before another tour of duty in a far away land.

The press had been briefed, and after a short session of questions and answers some of the soldiers were allowed to be interviewed and photographed. For some it was a way to say a final good-bye to family and friends. Others disappeared in the background opting for a quiet time alone.

Conner looked at his watch once again. He knew the reporters would soon be gone, closing the base from visitors for at least three weeks. He wanted to be part of the briefing; be involved somehow since the waiting was driving him crazy. The door opened as some of the officers began to enter the conference room. Each one nodded at him but he was more than aware of what they were thinking. It was unavoidable, Conner thought, feeling the stares of the newly arriving soldiers. He was not one of them, which made him either a civilian or a spook.

Conner looked at the window as the reporters were finally being led out from the staging area toward their cars. One thing Conner liked about the military; they were punctual. He knew that soon the twelve men in this room would step outside and brief their men.

"At ease gentlemen!" the booming voice of General William Walters, US Air Force, resonated around the room. His stride long and strong; Walters arrived at the podium before the men could react to his command.

"Please sit down," he said without a pause. "I want to formally welcome each one of you to Homestead. I know most of you arrived a few days ago; unfortunately I was away at the time. Hope you are all enjoying your stay in South Florida."

There were a few unintelligent comments, which both Walters and Conner ignored.

"First the obvious. This is a joint mission which will include Navy, Army, Marines, and, of course Air Force. The Navy's role will be more evident in the near future."

Some of the officers glanced in Conner direction once again.

"This is Mr. Conner; he will be overseeing certain part of this operation."

Conner said nothing.

"As of 1800 this base will be sealed from the outside world." Walters continued. "Your teams will have no communication, in or out of this base. In addition, you will not be departing tomorrow as scheduled."

Conner was not surprised at the looks the General was getting.

"All the actual hardware, meaning tanks, helicopters, missile systems, and munitions are being shipped ahead of time. Your men will spend at least two hours a day in simulators. We have acquired simulators for the AH-64 Apache Attack Helicopter and M-1 and M-2 tanks."

"Questions?" He did not wait for them. "Good."

"The men will be handed a bottle of suntan lotion to protect them from the South Florida sun. We need them to use it, but we also need them to make sure they get enough sun. We need them to tan but we want to make sure that they don't burn." Walters looked around for questions. "One more thing; everyone is to refrain from shaving until further noticed. That," he said sturdily. "It's an order."

The men seemed confused but nobody had any questions.

"Dismissed!" Walters said

Conner watched the men walking out of the room. Their faces seemed confused but they all knew to obey the orders. In a short period they will meet their squads and each will pass the orders as they saw fit.

Homestead was ready. There was only one more thing to take care of: Guantanamo.

Chapter 32

======================

"The blood of the infidel will flow—"

Conner raised his hand and the translator became silent. For almost an hour he had tried different approaches, trying to find a way to reach some part of this man but all he could see in his eyes was pure hatred.

"Leave us!"

The translator looked confused, "But how?"

"We'll manage," Conner said

The man hesitated but finally stood up after seeing no sign from Conner telling him to stay. The door closed, leaving Conner alone with Hanafar, his eyes still piercing into Conner's very soul.

"Any means..." the voice of Van Buren resonated in Conner's mind.

"Let's cut to the chase Abdul. You spent two years at Georgetown, followed by two more traveling all over the states; you should be able to understand me well enough."

The man said nothing

"For some reason, a wild college student who was happier drinking and screwing American girls than studying for his mid-term exams, turns into this holy man. A holy man whose idea of fun is killing innocent women and children."

Hanafar's mouth opened slightly

"I'm not interested in what you have to say." Conner stopped him from speaking. "All I need you to do is listen."

For the first time Conner notice the man blink.

"We have reasons to believe that someone is planning an attack on this base. Although we will be prepared, one of our biggest concerns is both your safety and—"

"You think the Cubans will attack your base?" Hanafar spat.

"Okay, let's say that's the case. What are we to expect from you?"

Hanafar returned to his silence.

"Oh come on! Everybody knows that you are revered as one of their spiritual leaders." Conner noticed his words were not reaching him. "Of course I wonder what they would think if we show them some home movies of you during your college years. You used to love to videotape yourself with all those girls didn't you?"

Again a blink.

"I need to know Abdul, what's going to happen if this camp gets hit?"

"We will kill every Americans or die trying!"

Conner stood up. "I guess I have my answer."

Hanafar watched Conner reached the door. "Don't you want to know why?" he asked.

Conner turned to him, his eyes looking dark and determined.

"Frankly I don't give a shit, but I'll tell you this. If even one of your friends out there plans or attacks a single American soldier, they will all die. I'll make sure of that myself. I don't care if that means poisoning all of you while you sleep."

Hanafar's eyes slowly looked away.

"The only thing is," Conner continued, his eyes enraged, his face getting in front of Hanafar's. "Nobody will touch you; instead you will be protected and taken care of until I arrive."

Hanafar's eyes were now looking down.

"You see Abdul, if one of your men touches a single soldier, I will make you my personal Jihad." Conner's hand was brandishing a small caliber gun that he was pressing directly against Hanafar's forehead. "You and your friends cannot imagine the type of torture I will submit you to."

Hanafar's was still feeling the gun pressed against his forehead. He tried unsuccessfully to make his lower lip stop trembling but he was too scared. All this time he knew that the Americans were full of idle threats, that even if they attacked them, they followed some kind of code, worrying too much about public opinion and the press; but not this man. "Please," he heard himself whimper.

The noise on the door made Hanafar open his eyes, realizing that Conner was no longer there.

"Cariño, dichosos los ojos que te ven," the female barkeep said as Navarro walked in. He was not surprised to hear her making a comment about not seeing him in so long. "Hey Angela."

"What do we owe the pleasure of your company?" she said bringing him a tin cup filled with beer. "That's all we have."

Navarro nodded and took a small sip, swallowing it immediately to avoid the taste. "Not bad," he lied.

"Yeah, right." She stood in front of him, moving closer. "So, what brings you here?"

"I'm looking for a man."

"Oh, no!" she almost shouted moving away. After looking around she returned to her original spot and drew herself close to him once again. "I lost too many friends after the attack on the palace, I am not getting involved."

Navarro said nothing; his hands remained wrapped around the tin cup, his eyes watching the bubbles of the drink.

"I thought they'd gotten you too," she said holding his hands.

"I lost many friends too, Angie. In fact I lost some really close friends." The look in his eyes was hiding a lot of hurt behind the strong determination. "He might be the one responsible for it."

Angela Rubio moved back trying to understand.

Navarro took a small picture and pushed it toward her. "His name is Eduardo Peralta. My best estimate is that he was working on both side and finally chose one." Navarro grabbed her hands and pulled her closer. "Angie, he is the one responsible for what happened to our friends."

"How do you know that?"

"I got it from more than one source."

He let go of her hands and she picked up the picture. "What do you want me to do?" she asked.

"I know you still have friends that can get you information. All I need is a location; I'll take care of the rest."

"What do you intend to do?"

"That's for me to decide, but let's just say that I will feel better."

Angela Rubio placed the picture in her pocket. "How do I contact you?"

"I'll be back next week. If you don't have anything, I'll find someone else."

"You'll get it," she said seriously.

Navarro reached over the counter and gave the woman a kiss on the cheek. "I know I will."

The conference room was bustling with activity, as Conner was lead in.

"Mr. Conner," Rear Admiral Daniels called waving him closer.

"Conner, this is Captain Mendez, and Lieutenant Carlton, who are in charge of our security. Captain Mendez is in charge of the Marines and Special Forces while Lieutenant Carlton handles the Army and ground weapons.

"Gentlemen," Conner nodded at the men.

Daniels continued with the introduction. "Captain Carpenter is in charge of the Air Force fighter wing that will be arriving shortly.

"Sir," Carpenter said at attention.

"Sergeant Bullock is overseeing all the cargo arriving. He will also be in charge of the maintenance until the other personnel arrives."

The sergeant nodded at Conner.

"And of course you know Captain Masterson."

"From *Enterprise*, yes I do." Conner shook the Captain's hand.

"Tell me Mr. Conner; are you the one responsible for that accident my ship is supposed to have?"

"No sir." Conner replied.

"Good," Masterson grunted.

"Unfortunately, some of our people have not returned from their briefing, however I believe we have everyone we need for your briefing." Daniels said pointing at the table.

The men stood next to their respective chairs waiting for Daniels to sit.

"Before we begin," Daniels said as everyone sat. "I want to advise you all about the press release that will be out tomorrow." Daniels passed a paper around. "We allowed a few reporters to tour the construction area for the new prisoner compound we are currently building. We feel that this would eliminate all the bad press we have received lately regarding prisoner housing. As the press toured the construction site, they were shown a design of a more hospitable facility. That is, in essence, how we will explain all the work being conducted at the base. The construction frame is nearly completed, which is what we need to house all troop and armament coming."

Daniels pressed a button and the middle of the conference table lit up with a detailed map of the base.

"As you all know, we have two subs currently patrolling the area around the base. Both USS Pasadena and San Juan will continue their patrol until this situation is resolved. Since the only Cuban vessels we should worry about are the Osa Class Patrol Boats, a strong attack will not come from the sea. We do have to worry about the *Osas* transporting troops but I think the two subs will be enough to neutralize any attacks."

Conner was listening carefully but his eyes were fixed on the map illuminating the table. As Daniels spoke, the map showed a representation of three *Osa* Patrol Boats being intercepted and destroyed by one of the submarines.

"Captain Masterson," Daniels said.

"Thanks, Admiral. Tomorrow afternoon *Enterprise* will be casting off from Guantanamo and the entire Strike Group will return to Norfolk. Of course *Enterprise* will have a sudden accident that will cripple her for a few days, forcing us to send all fighter planes away. I believe, Captain Carpenter, that this is when the Air Force fighter wing will arrive at Gitmo."

"Yes sir," Carpenter replied. "We feel that we can bring our F-15s into the base without arising any suspicions."

Masterson continued. "The Strike Group will continue to crawl north as the USS Washington's Strike Group will move east. This will continue for two days when *Washington's* Group will turn around. The Strike Group will position itself slightly southeast of the Florida Keys. In addition, the *Enterprise* Strike Group will join USS Washington, which will remain 60 miles east of the rest of her group. *Enterprise's* fighters will provide protection for both carriers.

If the Cuban planes leave Cuban waters, they will be intercepted by fighters from Boca Chica Naval Station and Homestead from the north and *Enterprise* and *Washington* from the east."

Conner could not help but compare the contrast this meeting had with the one he participated in Washington, when the discussion was about funding and politics.

"Lt. Carlton?" Daniels said.

"Sir, we have coordinated our efforts and Captain Mendez will speak for both."

Daniels nodded and turned to Mendez.

"The latest intel estimate a count of 30-40 tanks heading southeast, which we now believe will be in our general direction. This presents a problem since we have so much area to protect." Mendez pointed at an area in the map, which immediately began to grow. "The concentration of tanks will probably be heading to the northeast, around this entrance. We feel that this will be where they will concentrate most of their firepower for two reasons. One, the entrance on the northeast will allow their faster tanks to storm through and rapidly moved into the open area inside the base. Two, the recent replacement of mines by the Cubans near this entrance might indicate that the new mines could be dummies. If this is the case, they will have a few yard of open field for them to move forward." Mendez cleared his throat and continued. "No matter how fast our tanks can respond, they will be moving in by the time we can react, therefore we need to slow them down. We think that a few men, strategically hidden in the area with shoulder mounted systems can cause enough damage to slow them down."

"The 'Predators' are already here," Sergeant Bullock said.

"Truck bombs," Conner interrupted.

"I'm sorry sir," Mendez replied.

"Truck bombs. We could use two of the trucks and fill it with ordinance. Leave it casually near the entrance and detonate it as the tanks enter. It's worked in the Middle East for years." Conner shrugged. "Sorry for the interruption."

Mendez looked at Conner and then at Lt. Carlton. "That could work."

"Continue," said Daniels.

"Our biggest concern is the Hinds. Those gunships will cross with ease and probably attack our Command-and-Control center and these two other buildings. We will be able to slow them down with 'Stingers,' at least until the F-15s are airborne."

"The Eagles will be ready and manned since midnight on the 25th. We will be airborne in less than a minute." Carpenter said.

"Our other concerns are these two points here, and here." Mendez pointed at two areas in the map near the coast. Although the submarines will be patrolling, we feel that a smaller boat might get through. Our concern is an infiltration from Cuban Special Forces. We are moving our Navy Seals Team and Rangers down to these areas. In addition to the towers, we will have sentries searching the area. They will remain hidden not to attract attention." Mendez turned to Carlton. "Anything else Rob?"

"No. I think that we will adjust as the battle begins."

"Sergeant Bullock," Daniels said.

"Sir. All equipment is in position and ready for deployment. The transport planes will arrive tomorrow with the other personnel. Also, we will begin the evacuation of non-essential personnel very slowly, allowing a few families to leave with each plane."

Daniels nodded. "We need to continue our daily routine so a few families will stay behind until the last couple of days."

Bullock remained quiet until Daniels signaled for him to continue. "All operation will be moved to the town mall. Since the attack will be against the military installations, we will be able to conduct all operations from there. Command-and-Control will be moved to the McDonald's."

Bullock nodded abruptly and Daniels turned his attention to Conner.

"After your meeting with Hanafar, we feel that the situation will not be as explosive as we first feared; however we will implement some safeguards."

Conner said nothing.

"We are considering different ways to keep them mildly sedated since the night before. Even if they do not eat or drink on that night, we will find other ways to keep that area secure."

"Sir, if I may." Conner began.

"Go ahead, son."

"I think the Cubans know that if the prisoners were released in any way, you will have your hands full. An attack from the outside, while you are kept busy with the prisoners will be the type of situation they are looking for."

"I agree," Daniels said.

"So, a Special Force team, as Captain Mendez said, moving from this location could try to find a way to release the prisoners."

"We are aware of that, sir." Carlton said. "If a Special Force team lands on the base, that would most likely be their target."

Conner nodded. "But that could include the tanks as well. I mean they might be using the escape prisoners as part of the plan, be it through a covert operation or through their main attack. So even if we are prepared to intercept them. We have to make sure we are prepared to deal with the prisoners that escape."

"What are you suggesting?" Daniels asked.

"Even if it means destroying the entire camp; I think that we need to ensure our soldiers don't have to fight two enemies.

Daniels knew very well what Conner was trying to say. "Understood!"

Chapter 33

=================

The engines of two Navy C-40As came to a halt as each soldier stood at attention inside the empty hangar. Each officer stood next to his squad, waiting for the orders to board the planes. Although in the dark for the first few days, the officers now were aware of their current mission, something that will become very clear to each soldier.

General Walters arrived with the same determination as he did during their previous meetings.

"At ease gentlemen."

The noise of a forklift carrying a pallet full of boxes made everyone look towards the door.

"Before you ship out, there are a few things that need to be addressed." Walters seemed mellower than the officers had seen him in the past. "At this time, your gear is already waiting on your destination. You will not be going to the Middle East as per the original orders." Walters tried to hide a small hint of a smile.

"The good news is that your new destination is the Naval Base at Guantanamo, Cuba."

As he spoke, the boxes were being separated into different groups. It was hard for the group to ignore the activity behind Walters especially after the sudden news.

"The bad news however, is that you will be seeing action." Walters waited for the last two words to sink in. "I am not talking about the skirmishing you have been watching on the news as our fellow soldiers continue to police cities in the Middle East. I am talking about a large-scale attack, with an enemy that will be very determined and well armed. There will be casualties; you will be fighting against a larger force."

Walters noticed some of the men becoming restless.

"Your mission is to defend Gitmo at all cost against an attack that will occur in a week. The enemy's mission is clear, 'take full control of our base'. Your mission is to defend it. Is that understood?"

"Sir, yes sir!" the crowd shouted back.

"We have one major advantage over them," Walters continued. "In addition to the excellent men and women standing in front of me and currently in the base, we also have the element of surprise. We know that the attack is coming. We know when the attack is coming, but even more important, they don't know that you will be there waiting for them."

He looked back and noticed all the boxes were already in place.

"We need you to enter this camp, not as soldiers but as Prisoners of War. That was the reason why you were ordered to grow a beard and get a good South Florida tan. That is also why some of you were ordered to dye your hair yesterday."

A soft laughter was heard from some locations.

"In a few minutes you will be handed a uniform from those boxes. That is the uniform you will wear when you leave this hangar; that is the uniform you will wear when you arrive at Guantanamo. When you wear this uniform you are not to talk to anyone even if they are directly addressing you. Even if the goddamn President of the United States speaks to you; you are to continue walking, your eyes directly looking down at the floor."

The silence in the hangar was deafening.

"While in the plane you will be handed additional equipment to wear. You will follow the instructions given to you on the plane and you will not ask any questions. Understood?"

"Yes sir!"

"You will deplane in a single file and you will keep your head down until you are indoors and instructed otherwise. Once inside you will be allowed to shower and shave; something I'm sure most of you will do immediately."

There were a few more laughs.

"You and the people already in that base will make the difference in this fight. If we can pull this off, the enemy will have a big surprise waiting for them. The enemy doesn't know that you will be there waiting. They are not expecting the excellent fighting force that will be waiting for them. They are not expecting YOU to be there!"

The men were slowly beginning to get more animated.

"You are one fighting force, you are prepared to defend your country not to police a street in some godforsaken land. In this mission you will be fighting, you will be defending your country and when the time comes you will show our enemy that their idea of superiority is nothing compared to the might of the US Armed Forces. Is that understood?"

"Sir, yes sir!" The soldiers shouted as Walters's men began to pass around the red jumpsuits.

"Dismissed!" Walters shouted. "And give 'em hell!"

Chapter 34

==================

"I don't wanna leave daddy!"

Lt. Commander Anderson grabbed his little girl and spun her around in a big circle. "You have to, sweetie."

"But why?"

Jenny Anderson picked the girl from her husband's arm. "Come on Emily, we have to start getting ready."

"But why do we have to go?" Emily cried out.

"Because we're going to see grandma," her mother answered.

"And why can't daddy come?"

"Daddy will be there in a few days, Emi."

Anderson tried not to show the worry in his face. "I need to take care of some things first. Besides, the planes are only for mommies and kids."

Emily pouted trying to get her father to feel bad. She did not know how awful he was already feeling letting the two women in his life leave.

"Come on Emily," he whispered, reaching for her once again. "Let's get some ice-cream before you leave.

The C-40 taxied near the new, recently arrived, prefabricated buildings that would provide housing for the new "inmates" arriving into the base. Marines, M-16's ready, surrounded the walk from the transports to the barbwire section.

The newly arrived "prisoners" began to descend the C-40 in a single line. Their walk was difficult due to the chains connecting each prisoner's leg to one another. Some had their face covered; others walked slowly looking directly to the ground.

"Williams? Is that you?" A Marine turned in shock toward one of the prisoners walking slowly to the complex.

The man paid no attention as he continued his somber walk.

"Williams, it's me Randal."

Randal felt a hand on his shoulder. He turned around startled to see the sturdy face of his commanding officer.

"Sir!"

"Walk away Marine."

"But sir."

"Stand down, Marine!"

The young Marine stepped away, his eyes glued to the back of a prisoner he had come to know as Lieutenant Williams.

"Los pobres," Sgt. Menendez said; his binocular fixed at the scene playing across the bay. As one of the Cuban soldiers carefully watching the current scene in the American base, Menendez could not help but feel sorry for the recent arrivals.

"Why do you call them 'poor souls'?" the soldier next to him asked.

"They are prisoners; they are probably going to spend years in that prison until the Yankees decide what to do with them."

"Bah, to them it will be a great improvement. The closest thing those people ever had to a home is a cold cave with rats as food. In fact I'm willing to bet that those men will eat better than us."

"How could you say that?" Menendez said angrily.

"Oh, shove it kid; you know it's true. Look at the plane they brought them in; it's the same type that usually transport their own people."

Menendez ignored the man, concentrating on the prisoners moving slowly into their future home.

"Mommy!" Emily shouted; her mouth full of chocolate.

"How do I look?" Jenny Anderson asked posing.

"Why are you wearing a uniform, mommy?"

Lt. Commander Anderson walked to his wife and kissed her. He turned back to his daughter and picked her up from her chair. "Mommy is playing a game; and pretty soon you are going to play one too."

"Really? Cool!" Emily Anderson shouted.

Anderson grabbed a napkin and wet it, cleaning his daughter's mouth.

A knock on the door startled them.

Anderson walked to the door and opened it.

A quiet looking Marine was standing in front of his door, the engine of the car behind him still running. "Sorry sir, it's time."

Emily began to pout once again as her father kissed her on the forehead. "Now sweetie, you know this has to happen."

"I know daddy, but I don't want to leave you."

"I know but I promise I'll be there in just a few days. Besides, you are going to play the game soon."

Emily hugged her father. "So what's the game?"

"Well," he said whispering in her ear while pointing at the quiet Marine by the door. "This man is going to take you and mommy to the place where the planes are."

"And?"

"And…they're going to hide you in a large box."

"That's no fun," Emily frowned.

"Actually it is because all the other kids are going to hide too. The one that is the quietest is going to get a toy. Isn't that right sergeant?"

"Yes sir."

Emily was suddenly more interested in the game. "Cool!"

Jenny Anderson grabbed Emily away from her husband but the little girl pulled away from her mother, her hands wrapping around her father's neck. "I'm gonna miss ya daddy."

"Me too sweetie," Anderson said kissing her again.

Jenny pulled and Emily finally let go of her father. "You promised you would tell me what this is all about."

"I will," Anderson said. "As soon as I see you again; I'll tell you."

Jenny kissed her husband good-bye as the Marine started walking away with her suitcase.

"Gentlemen," Van Buren called as he stood up from behind his desk. "Something I can help you with."

The young aide began to speak.

"I believe this is between Mr. Van Buren and me, Anthony," the Secretary of Defense said.

"Yes, sir."

"Leave us," the old man said turning his attention to Van Buren.

The young aide moved quickly across the room, closing the door behind them.

"Sir, let me remind you that—"

"I know. Anything said in this office will be recorded. Frankly, I am too old to care any longer."

Van Buren turned and pressed a button. Behind him a small light illuminated a panel, now visible to his guest.

The Secretary of Defense paid no attention to the equipment now being displayed. "As I said, I am too old, but thank you."

Van Buren nodded in return. He knew that the recorder on his desk was still detecting every single noise in the entire office.

"Your protégé seems very intelligent, although a little rough around the edges."

"He'll come around," Van Buren responded. "Besides, I don't think this is the reason why you're paying me a visit."

"Not unlike his teacher," the old man remarked. "Very well. As you know, we've had a headache in Guantanamo for a few years. Every week we have complaints from the Red Cross, activists, foreign powers, and high price lawyers, all of which have nothing better to do than question the treatment of the prisoners in Camp Delta, or X-Ray, or whatever it's called right now."

Van Buren remained quiet.

"They no longer seem to care that most of those people were terrorist, sworn to attack this country at all cost. It's hard to understand how quickly they forget."

"There hasn't been an attack—"

"Of course not! We took the war back to them. We had them running and hiding instead of finding ways to attack us. We have our young men and women dying in a pile of shit of a country so that no one dies here."

"I know this as well as you do sir; but that's not how it is reported," Van Buren agreed.

"I know that! If we had one of the terrorists that were in one of the planes during 9/11; there would still people protesting about the way they are being treated."

Van Buren said nothing.

"This attack on Guantanamo, I think it's a blessing in disguise. Something both the current administration and the one to follow could appreciate."

Van Buren relaxed back in his chair. He knew exactly what the Secretary of Defense was trying to say. The old man, however would have to spell it out to him, including the fact that this was an order. "Go on."

Chapter 35

==================

"That's strange," Menendez said; his binoculars fixed on the incoming fighters.

"What is it now?" Figueroa, the older soldier, asked annoyed.

"The American fighters that are landing. They're not F-14s. I think they're F15s."

"Fourteen, fifteen, what's the difference?"

"The difference," Menendez said looking back at the old man sitting in his post not paying attention at the world around him. "The difference is that the F-14 is an old American Navy plane, the F-15 is Air Force."

"So?"

"So, according to our instructions the planes that should be arriving are Navy F-14s and F-18s."

"Give me that," the old man grunted pulling the binoculars away from the kid. He took a quick look at the two new planes rapidly disappearing behind the trees that hid the runway. "They don't look armed."

"Well, they are, at least the ones I've seen," the kid replied.

"Isn't that what the instructions were, to make sure the planes were not armed?"

"Yes, but—"

"Be quiet," the old man protested turning his attention to the diagram of the two planes that were handed to him a few hours ago. "Looks the same to me."

Menendez took the binoculars once again and began searching the sky for more planes.

"You think we should report this?" he asked the old man.

"Report what? Just watch the planes land and make sure nothing else happens." He sat back on the chair and closed his eyes. *If only I could shut that bloody radio,* he thought looking at the younger man's radio currently broadcasting a speech.

He had been speaking for over two hours, yet he showed no signs of ending.

Domingo Maldonado sat next to Raul Castro as Fidel continued his speech. Maldonado was not really listening at the moment; instead his mind went over all the different scenarios that will play out soon. None of them had a positive outcome.

"Everything in place?" Raul whispered.

"On schedule," Maldonado whispered back. "General Guerra has taken over the installation in Santa Clara."

"Very good," Raul said.

"So, what is troubling you?" Maldonado asked.

"I sympathize with my brother, I too would like to see the American base flying the Cuban flag, and I know that for a few hours, it will. The problem is that once the Americans retaliate we will not have anywhere to go."

"He will not approve."

"My brother wants to destroy Miami, and I too want that nest of Cuban '*escoria*' eliminated. The attack on Miami will bring retaliation, especially after our second attack. My brother knows that the attack will guarantee his death, as he will fight until his last breath." Raul turned suddenly to face Maldonado. "I do not want to lose control of Cuba that way."

"What are you suggesting?"

"I want you to contact some of our friends in Colombia and Venezuela. Advise them that we might need to seek refuge for a few days."

"Are you suggesting?"

"No," Raul tried not to raise his voice. "I want the best for my brother and I will not allow him to die losing control of this island. I want to take him away, as the attack begins. When the Americans retaliate, we will surface from where we are, chastising whoever was responsible for it."

"Are you serious about this?"

"Dead serious. My brother deserves better than to lose all he's fought for so long on the moment of his death."

"He will not agree to this."

"Let me worry about that." Raul replied. "Make the arrangements."

Now, I have some great news. As you all know our patriotic forces will be flying to Venezuela to help their government keep the stability in that country. A peaceful country that has fallen into turmoil and it is now in the brink of civil war. And why, do you ask? Because of the influence of the Mafia, the Cuban Mafia in Miami that continues to influence and manipulate the American government and now is trying to extend its propaganda to some of our allies.

But that... that is no longer important.

Our friends in Venezuela are paying us in many ways, but most of all, they are paying us in a way that you will experience soon. This coming Independence Day we will have a celebration like you have never seen before.

Beginning at noon on July 25, we will close all our businesses, all factories, all schools and we will begin our celebration. A celebration that will last the entire weekend. A celebration in which the beer and rum will flow like you had not seen before. This will be a party like no other.

The crowd cheered, but not like so many times in the past, when the applauses seemed staged. This time the cheering seemed genuine, the applause thunderous and unrehearsed.

The speech was now almost three hours long as Conner sat watching the man's every move. The feed, captured from one of the signals broadcasting across the island, was redirected to the farmhouse in Homestead. Delayed by almost 20 minutes, the speech now included subtitles in Spanish. In addition, a 'scroll bar' on the right side of the screen pointed at upcoming sections of the speech with some significance.

Conner was not listening to the words. Although he could understand every word being said, Conner's attention was in the body language of the man giving the speech.

He was ignoring Dexter, who was sitting next to a computer screen, monitoring the feed and the programs translating the information while listening through a pair of headphones. Only Conner knew that he was not really listening to the speech, instead he was probably playing some heart-pounding techno music.

Conner was also ignoring Becker, who was reading every single caption on the screen. Even though the next significant section would not appear for another 7 minutes, Becker continued to read every word.

Conner's eyes were fixed on the screen, watching carefully every move. It was the first time, since the attack on the palace, that Conner had a chance to study the man. It was probably the only opportunity he would have.

The phone calls had quiet down, as well as the visits. For the first time in weeks Conner was sitting in a comfortable couch watching television. Granted it was work but it was restful work. The hard part was done, all their findings were given to the military; the job was now theirs. They were meeting daily with military intelligence but the size of the meetings was shortening as the date neared.

There was one thing that still troubled Conner and this was the reason why he was studying the man so carefully.

Conner's main question continued to remain unanswered: **why?**

Watching him, Conner could not understand why this calculating man would suddenly decide to attack the US. For years he has been the target of numerous CIA plots, some to destroy him, others to ridicule him. None succeeded.

Even when he seemed to be losing control of a situation, the man always found a way to turn it around to his advantage. He could be called many things but Conner knew that this man was extremely intelligent. That was what troubled Conner. *Why would he give it all up just for a suicide attack?*

The answer was in front of him, and Conner realized it for the first time.

"Freeze it!" he shouted at Dexter but the man could not hear him. "Dexter!" he shouted once again.

Becker threw a piece of ice at Dexter making the man look up. "What?"

"Back up about ten seconds," Conner said.

Dexter pressed a button and the picture moved back slowly.

"There, stop it right there." Conner said.

The picture remained frozen as Dexter stood next to Conner. "What is it boss?"

"Look at his face, his eyes."

Dexter looked at the screen and back to Conner in confusion.

Becker however began to notice. "He looks like he is in pain."

"Yes," Conner said. "A lot of pain." He turned to Dexter and asked him to move the picture a few frames. "Look, the pain is almost agonizing there."

"I hadn't notice," Becker said.

"I nearly missed it. At first I thought it was just my imagination but this time it was more obvious. It seems like it is getting worse."

Dexter continued the feed but did not return to his music. "So what do you think?" he asked Conner.

"The falls and disappearance in the past few months were attributed to age. We knew about it and we knew that he had been sick; but it was all routine stuff. Still, all along his mind has remained sharp." Conner signaled Dexter to continue with the feed. "All this time I've been trying to figure out why this sudden attack? Why now? What would he accomplish by this attack? The answer is now in front of us."

Dexter continued to be confused.

Becker was not. "You mean he might be dying?"

A small alarm went off and Dexter ran to the computer. "Speech's over," he said.

Becker's attention returned to Conner. "Why would you think that?"

"He never had a reason to attack us. In fact he has remained pretty quiet lately, and then, all of a sudden he decides to do this. Why?"

"I know but dying?"

"Yes, dying. He knows that this would be a futile attack, not unlike the Moncada Barrack back in his youth. It's the beginning and the end."

Becker remained silent.

"Think about it. Dying, something that he has no control over it, unless—"

"He attacks us, and we retaliate."

"Killing him in the process. The man will die on July 26th, the date that means more to him than any other date." Conner added.

Dexter's eyes grew larger. He was confused but the conversation made sense.

"Dying on July 26th, that's brilliant," Becker said.

"Those who follow him will remember the day in happiness for the revolution and sadness for his death. Those who hate him will remember this day in anger for what it represents, not to mention the attack on Miami."

"And yet," Becker added. "They will have to celebrate this date for his death."

The feed continue as the speech came to a close. *...And as I said to Celia in my letter back in June 5, 1958...*

"And that," Conner said pointing at the words. "Is the signal!"

Chapter 36

====================

"Continue," Fidel Castro said.

The head of intelligence nodded and turned to the map once again.

The room was quiet, only the head of intelligence had been allowed in for the past week. Although there were thousands involved in the current mobilization; no general or admiral had spoken to Fidel or Raul since the decision was made to have Maldonado as liaison officer between the brothers and the armed forces. Raul, the supreme leader of all the Cuban armed forces, was too busy 'organizing' the mobilization of Cuban forces to Venezuela.

"At 4:00 AM tomorrow morning our planes will take off from here, here and here," Maldonado said pointing at airports in the northeast of the island.

"Targets?" Raul said, knowing well enough what the answer was.

"The first strike team is to attack the bases at Cayo Hueso and Homestead. This will keep their planes on the ground. We estimate that the Baracoa force should be able to take care of that."

Fidel nodded picking a cigar from a box and smelling it.

"Ten minutes after the planes take off; two new waves will depart from here, and here. The force from Varadero is to maintain air superiority; in case any American plane does take off."

Raul was about to say something but Maldonado cut him. "We also have to take into consideration any planes from *Enterprise*. We're aware that the carrier is limping to its home port but we are not sure if any planes remained on the ship."

"What about the planes in Guantanamo?"

"I think that by the time Guantanamo finds out what is happening in the US, they will be too busy to render any assistance."

Fidel nodded. "Top priority, airports and air superiority. Continue."

"Our main targets are, the Freedom Tower, Our Lady of Charity Church, Little Havana, of course."

"Of course," Raul replied.

Maldonado continued pointing out the targets, all known Cuban interest in the US. Each target represented either a landmark or symbol of Cuban success in the new country. The targets were corporations and homes owned by well-known Cubans, as well as other interests.

"You forgot a target," Fidel said. "I don't see the 'Hermanos Al Rescate' base."

Maldonado smiled. "I thought it would be a nice surprise; of course we have the 'Brothers to the Rescue' hangar as a target."

Castro smiled, finally lighting up the cigar. "Going back to Guantanamo?"

"Our tanks will be ready by 4:00 AM but no shots will be fired until 4:30. We want to make sure the planes have reached and destroyed the target before we begin our land campaign."

"So what is the solution for braking into the American Base," Fidel asked Raul. "What have you finally decided?"

"Between 3:00 AM and 3:30 two teams will infiltrate the base from the south. One team will concentrate on the camp known as 'Camp X-Ray,' while the other team will move into the new camp on the east side of the bay. The team's main objective is to open up the camps at whatever cost.

We foresee that the men will be ready by the time the tanks make their move. This way the base will be attacked from the outside as well as the inside. We are not worried about providing the prisoners with weapons, since we're only counting on them as a diversionary tactic."

"Yet, they might attack the same people who liberated them," Fidel argued.

"I know, my brother. The men are ex-Spetnaz, the best Special Forces the Soviet Union ever had. They know the risk."

"Continue," Fidel said.

"There will be a line of about 12 tanks that will not cross into the base. These tanks will concentrate all the firepower on the closest targets, which includes some of the barracks and one of the main buildings. The barrage will create confusion at first but the Americans will respond by moving to that location.

The remaining tanks will advance and cross into the base from the northeast entrance. The entrance is usually quiet and only defended by a few soldiers who would not stand a chance against our tanks moving in. At the same time the assault helicopters will move in to help the advancing tanks. As the tanks enter the base, the remaining 12 tanks will be mobilized as well."

Castro puffed a large circle of smoke.

"The Americans will be concentrating on the attack from the north, and of course pulling back," Maldonado added.

"At the same time, two of our transport will land on their own airport, escorted by assault helicopters. If all goes according to plan, our special forces will provide ground support as well."

"What if the team fails?" Castro asked watching the smoke rise.

"If the team fails, the tanks are ordered to hit the prisoners' camp. We estimate that there will be casualties, but as I said before, those prisoners will serve as a diversionary target." Raul pointed at a new location in the map. "While the chaos continues, we will bring ships from the east and west of the base and attack their flanks. Guantanamo will collapse to us."

"Enough details," Fidel said. "You know that not everything goes according to plans; therefore I have two questions."

"Yes, my brother," Raul said.

"The second wave?"

"They will be fueled and ready. Although, if the Americans do react, our older planes will not stand a chance against them. They will, however, give the 29s chance to land and refuel if needed."

"Very well, what about our other little surprise?"

Raul continued. "The missiles are ready. Guerra is in charge and he will await your order. As soon as our planes return and the Americans fighters are deployed from other bases all our missiles will be fired, including our two tactical ones."

"Most of those missiles have a range of 40-50 kilometers, they will crash in the water," Maldonado added. "But of course, they will give the American pilots enough of a headache to allow for the tactical ones to break through."

"Very well," Fidel said. "I guess all we have to do now is wait."

Juan Navarro sat quietly in the park bench while people danced and celebrated. To everyone around him he was probably too drunk to celebrate any more for the night. The party had started at noon in most of the workplaces and by 2:00 PM the offices were closing down as everyone began to take the celebration to the streets. Small towns closed their main street for their celebrations while some of the larger cities had arranged different locations for the parties; it was Mardi Gras and *Calle* 8 wrapped into one.

Angela's friends were very good and Navarro got his answer as expected. That was the reason why he was sitting on the park bench, waiting. Navarro closed his eyes and tried to control himself. He could feel the anger surging through his veins, the need for revenge slowly consuming him.

He could never admit he loved Marcie, in fact their relationship, although sexual at times was more a partnership than a love affair. He taught her how to be more careful and patient, she showed him to open up and to trust again.

Navarro showed her the ropes, all the tricks of living under Communism. To the rest of the world terrorism was the threat. The old Cold War tactics were long gone…but not in this country.

But this was now; this was the night before the impending attack. This was the night were Cuba celebrated and danced like it had not done before.

To people the celebration was one of the few things they could do to forget everything else in their lives. July 26 was not only the most revered date in Castro's Cuba; it was also Christmas, New Years, and any other celebration possible. It wasn't important if you supported the regime; a party was a party and they welcomed the celebration with open arms.

Navarro could smell the beer that he purposely spilled on his shirt before he sat on the bench. His mouth could taste the beer that was so hard to get but was flowing so freely today. It was a rare occasion; something that nobody seemed to question and he wondered if he would have, had he not known what would soon be happening.

But no, his mind should return to the task at hand, watching the building across from where he was sitting, the building that housed the man he was looking for. The man he had been waiting to see for almost four hours.

As if in response to his wishes, Peralta finally stepped out of the door of the building and started to walk.

Navarro crossed the street without looking. There were seldom any cars in Cuba and on a day like today; nobody wanted to drive, instead everyone was in the streets.

It was only after a block and a half that Navarro caught up with his target.

"Eduardo!" Navarro shouted.

Peralta turned without hesitation. This was his neighborhood; he knew most of the people here but the man staggering toward him was a stranger.

"Do I know you?"

"It's me," Navarro said. "Juan, Maria's friend..." The name might mean nothing to Peralta but Navarro would bet that Peralta would know at least one Maria.

"Maria?" Peralta asked allowing Navarro to get closer.

Navarro threw his arm around his target in a friendly gesture, his breath making Peralta turn his face.

"I know many women named Maria," Peralta said. "Maria who?"

"You know," Navarro said pulling the man suddenly into a quiet dark alley.

Peralta never saw the blade; in fact he didn't even feel it piercing his skin. The pain reached him almost at the same time as Navarro's voice.

"Maria Cecilia Fernandez," Navarro said twisting the knife inside the man's stomach. "You were the man who gave the order to have her killed."

Navarro removed the knife and quickly raised it, slitting the man's throat. The original wound might not kill Peralta but this one will. He would not be able to yell for help; instead he would slowly drown in his own blood. He knew this well; he had done it too many times to know how it happens.

Navarro moved back slightly, watching Peralta's eyes filling up with blood as the man watched him in horror, gasping for air. "Marcie sends her regards *hijo de puta*!" Navarro nearly shouted, his hand still holding the knife, waiting, even hoping for the man to move. His hand was looking for an excuse to use the blade once again.

Two women passed by the corner, singing out loud and dancing to a distant song, too drunk to realize how out of tune they were.

Navarro, having cleaned his blade on Peralta's shirt moved quickly behind them. As the women reached the next corner, Navarro caught up with them.

He didn't have to ask, within seconds Navarro had his arms around them as the trio crossed the street, dancing and singing through the streets of Havana.

The figure on the portrait stood proud and heroic. A recognizable face, it had somehow stood the test of time becoming an icon for those who fought against the system. To some he had been a hero, a revolutionary, even a martyr. To others he had been a gangster, a killer, and a terrorist. The older generation had an opinion on him; good or bad, they knew of the man. Young people liked the picture, and some, feeling a hint of rebellion associate themselves with what he represented never understanding who he truly was.

The portrait loomed in the darkness as a lonely man stood in front of it as he did so many times in the past.

"Che," he spoke softly. "Mi hermano, how many times have I wondered how different things would've been if you had stayed."

The portrait remained silent, the image smiling back at the shell of a man that was once a young warrior fighting alongside him.

"I understand now why you left, why you couldn't stay here. Your soul could not sit idle and govern a country. You needed to continue the fight. You always wanted to be in the action; fighting, making the revolution yours." A trail of smoke spiraled upward from the old man as he moved closer to the picture.

"It was so different for me." Fidel was looking directly at the picture, his eyes meeting the eyes of the man who died so long ago.

"It became so easy to sit and be in control of everything. It became so...natural."

The smoke danced around the portrait distorting the face; at times making it seem alive.

"I now understand your reasons for leaving; I finally know why you wanted to continue the fight."

A breeze sneaked through one of the windows blowing the smoke away.

"You always wanted to take the fight back to the Yankees. Even as you died, you fought them to the last breath. I now understand what you were trying to do."

He put the cigar down; let it sit on the desk as he stood in attention in front of the picture.

"My brother, tomorrow I will join you. Tomorrow I too will die fighting the imperialists"

The man moved softly away after a perfect military salute.

Chapter 37

================

Hold! The voice on the com-link came to life making Captain Kristopher James raise his fist immediately. The three other member of the team stopped behind him, the darkness serving as their only ally.

3,2,1…

The body of a young militiaman slumped in front of James, a bullet hole on the right side of his head.

Clear. The voice on the com-link announced.

"No shit!" James heard a voice from behind.

The team began to move closer to the door. James knew that his sniper was watching their every move closely.

Two more on the roof.

"Take them," James replied as he introduced the tiny optic cable under the door of the small bunker. He raised two fingers, immediately pointing at the directions where the two men inside were located.

The optic cable was removed and immediately the door burst open.

The two militiamen inside turned expecting to see their comrade come in and complain once again on the party they were missing. They were dead wrong.

Two bursts secured the room as the com-link came alive once again. ***Roof cleared!***

"Bunker secured," James answered back. "Ready for Team #2."

The sniper raised a finger and four men began their decent down the small hill. They crossed the clearing and entered the bunker. James turned and began giving orders.

"You two, on the roof; I don't want any surprises."

The men moved immediately and disappeared from view.

"Mark, Luis, I want you to take care of our guest here," James said looking at one of the members of team #2. "Kid, do your magic."

The trio ran outside and also disappeared.

James turned to his lieutenant and told him to stay put. After announcing on the com-link to his "eyes" to keep watch, he moved swiftly outside with his last member.

The bunker was well hidden, surrounded by a cañaveral, or sugar cane field from three different locations. A small hill on the south hid part of the compound, as well as the road leading to it from the southeast.

The area was small, used only to house the soldiers in charge of the four V-75 Surface-to-Air missiles still sitting on the rear side of the bunker. This was of no concern to James and his team. Neither was the large radar dish on the southwest corner of the compound.

The reasons for their infiltration were cradled in two large trucks directly facing south. As James stepped out of the bunker he noticed the young SEAL working on one of the two Soviet SS-22 missiles, the missiles that according to their intel were carrying a 50-kiloton nuclear warhead each.

James knew only two things about the weapons.

With a range of almost 800 kilometers, their target could be anywhere in the southeastern side of the US.

The warheads would devastate most, if not an entire city.

He shook the vision from his mind and began to run toward the small dirt road. He needed to be prepared for an attack; an attack that could only come from that road.

Lieutenant Blanco opened the Cuban newspaper sitting on a corner table. There was nothing he could do but wait; to all intent and purposes the mission had been a piece of cake.

The loud ring of a telephone made him jump in his boots

"Oh shit!" he cursed. "Captain we have a problem!"

The air felt muggy and damp but the team continued to move easily across the base making good time. They were expected to reach the new detention center close to 3:00 AM, but it had taken them less than two hours to reach the west side of the runway.

Captain Orestes Delgado was amazed at the ease in which the team moved across the base. The first hour they encounter almost no patrols making one of his men wonder if the base was deserted. The second hour was slightly more difficult but again the team found very little activity. The few patrols in the area seemed to be moving away from their direction. Delgado thought that they seriously overestimated the American security force. Either that or the Americans were avoiding them.

The four-man team stopped west of the runway in a small covered area. Delgado knew they were too early and without any way to communicate with the other team, they had to wait. They had a schedule to follow, it was the way it was planned and rehearsed. They could not deviate.

Delgado looked at his watch once again wondering the location of Quintana's team. His long-time friend, Quintana was in charge of the other team, now moving closer to old prisoner's camp.

The original plan was to have both teams attack the prison, allowing for more prisoners to be liberated. With the addition of the camp on the western part of the base, a new plan was designed.

The new camp was built as a processing area, allowing the prisoners to remain isolated for a few days before the move to Delta. Unfortunately for the Americans, the arrival of new prisoners and the overcrowded conditions of Camp Delta forced the newly built area to become a prison as well.

A patrol was moving near their location and Delgado looked back quickly to make sure his team was in place. The vehicle accelerated past them, the soldiers inside not bothering to even look in their direction.

Delgado was slightly worried about the open area in front of him. The distance from his current location to the runway was roughly 150 yards, a distance that was fully in the open. Delgado originally thought of crossing the area if they were late, arriving early he only stopped to allow his men to rest. Now it was time to move.

The north side of the runway was perfect for his team. Between bushes, palm trees and small sheds, they would have no problem in covering the area with ease. The mission required for them to be unseen, and to avoid any confrontation. They were to rig the charges and hide once again. Once the attack began; the explosion would allow all the prisoners to escape. It was simple really; the base will be attacked from land, sea, air, and from within.

"Let's move," Delgado whispered. The men moved swiftly, disappearing into the darkness.

Conner watched as the Gulfstream disappeared in the distance.

"Well, here we are." Becker said turning back to Conner who remained motionless. The Gulfstream was Van Buren's last attempt to evacuate Conner and Becker from South Florida, but they both refused.

The rest of the team was gone. Tamargo never returned after his visit from Cuba and Dexter left two days before, taking all the equipment with him. Hawkins was in Hawaii with agent Murray, helping her capture one of the six Cubans the FBI was investigating. After the speech from Castro, the man bought a one-way ticket to Hawaii, something that made both Murray and Hawkins very interested. The other five Cubans had been arrested but the sixth man continued to slip away from the FBI traps.

Henderson flew his family away for the weekend while he remained behind. It was a hard thing to do, saying goodbye to this family, wondering if he would ever see them again.

"Come on," Conner finally said. "Let's go."

The duo turned and began to walk back to the buildings. Not far from them, fighters were moving into position, the pilots ready for the orders to take off.

Delgado's team reached the north end of the runway when they stopped suddenly. From their previous location, they were unable to see their target. Hidden in darkness, the camp was almost invisible, even under their 'night enhancement' goggles. It was a strange sight, a prisoner camp that was shrouded in darkness, almost invisible to everyone. Delgado could not understand why the camp would be so dark, until now.

"What the hell?" One of his men said.

Side by side, the buildings looked more like one large warehouse than the separate small 'prefab' houses that Delgado read in his report.

This was not the cause for the team's reaction.

The sight in front of them was that of a large warehouse. A warehouse that in complete darkness was currently full of activity. Through the goggles, Delgado could see the American tanks and helicopters, hidden inside the warehouse. Around them, men were hurriedly preparing the equipment, as others prepared to board them.

Even more alarming, the unarmed fighters that landed only days ago were now fully armed with missiles and bombs as pilots sat in the cockpits waiting.

They know! Delgado's mind shouted not truly noticing the noise behind him. At first he thought a large mosquito had zipped through his ear; but the loud thud next to him made him look back; two of his men collapse immediately followed by another.

Delgado ignored the men who were now lying dead next to him. He knew this was a trap, he knew a bullet would soon be coming for him. His hands were shaking as he fumbled for his radio. *Have to warn them, have to warn them!*

The small flash of light in the distance caught his attention. It was a tiny flicker, but one that register much brighter in his mind. Just as sudden, without feeling pain, or fear, or regret, his mind registered total darkness.

Chapter 38

==================

USS Enterprise's demise was greatly exaggerated.

Not long after leaving Guantanamo, *Enterprise* was crippled by a large fire. The fire began with a ruptured fuel tank on one of the old F-14 Tomcat and spread almost immediately. As her crew spent hours combating a fire that almost reached one of its nuclear reactors, 'Big E' tried to limp its way back to port. The rest of the strike group remained with her as *Enterprise* evacuated the fighters to different locations.

That was the official report.

The news coverage continued to bring experts to analyze the status of the old aircraft carrier and the danger it represented to the east Atlantic. While some argued that the ship was too old for the amount of action it had seen in the Middle East, others argued about the validity of nuclear carriers.

Reports arrived on the following day that the reactor was never in danger, something that made most of the news organization extremely unhappy.

Hours later, *Enterprise*, still trailing smoke, began to move slowly back to her homeport. A Russian satellite confirmed all the news reports, its pictures finding a way to the Cuban Interest Section in Washington DC.

Two days later, USS Enterprise was no longer newsworthy. The whereabouts of the USS Washington were unknown.

After the training exercise with *Enterprise*, the carrier group was to steam into the Mediterranean Sea where *Washington* would join the USS Truman's Strike Group.

With *Washington* gone and *Enterprise* now slowly limping north, Cuba concentrated all their fighters strike capability on only two military targets: Key West and Homestead.

Unbeknown to the forces in the island, both *Washington* and *Enterprise* were prepare to move swiftly back to their intended location. Early evening on July 25, both carriers were in position.

Slightly northeast of Cuba, *Enterprise's* Strike Group joined USS Washington. With a 50-mile no fly zone around them, the ships were now combat ready. All they had to do now was wait.

Captain Masterson paced on the bridge as he did before any maneuvers, be it war games or real confrontation. This time he was more uncomfortable than ever. If his men failed, his country would be attack, not by terrorist using unconventional weapons, but by a military enemy using the same tactics and weapons he had studied and applied so many times.

"Sir, we need to bring the patrols in soon."

Masterson turned almost immediately. "Have them come immediately. In the meantime, launch extra fighters. I have a feeling we're going to be seeing action soon."

"Sir?"

The shout of a crewman made everyone turn. "Hawkeye reports two, no five contacts."

"It starts," he thought as the word was given for general quarters.

Captain Mariano Abreu engaged the afterburner in his Mig-29 as the plane reached 3,000 feet. There was no real reason to climb any further; his target was only minutes away. The radar continued to show activity, as more Cuban fighters joined him in his current course.

"Just a walk in the park," he muttered to himself feeling his body tense up slightly as the plane pushed him back against the seat.

Abreu smiled as he noticed the silhouette of another plane next to him, which he identified immediately as Rigoberto Rivera's plane. His friend and wingman, Rivera always liked to fly next to him, often pushing him to the limit. This time there would be no game, no race;

this time they would go side-by-side and deliver their cargo to the Americans.

The mission called for complete radio silence, something he agreed on absolutely during the briefing. At this point however, he wished the orders had been different. He needed to hear Rivera's voice, needed his sense of humor. Looking again at his friend's plane, he could slightly distinguish the man, probably making some kind of obscene gesture back at him.

American water, he thought trying to calm his nerves. The radar showed contacts ahead but Abreu paid little attention to them. They were briefed that there will be multiple ground contacts. The coast of the Florida Keys will be filled with cruise ships and large boats due to weekend activities.

His attention however was slowly moving to the air traffic activity that was beginning to appear at long range.

"What is this?" Abreu asked himself trying to figure out the bleeps appearing and disappearing on his screen.

Within seconds his radar changed drastically. The three bleeps that he saw only seconds ago disappeared, only returning with hundreds of bleeps representing targets all around his aircraft and immediately disappearing.

He looked back at his friend's plane and began to make gestures for Rivera to look back but his wingman seemed busy, probably checking his systems before the attack.

Maybe the radar is malfunctioning, he thought. It wasn't the first time his plane has given him radar trouble in the past. He exhaled deeply and checked his radar again. *Damn!*

Most of the first strike team was now in the Florida Straight; all moving without triggering any alarms.

Mariano could see the lights of Cayo Hueso ahead. The trip had taken less than he expected.

The alarms in his plane came to life making Abreu panic. *Missile lock? Where?*

According to his plane's warning system, one of the boats had a missile lock on him. Abreu looked furiously around, trying to find some kind of a sign.

He turned to his friend's plane and noticed that Rivera's fighter was beginning a rapid climb. Abreu pulled on his stick and started to climb as well.

Rivera was ahead of him as the alarm continued. The cockpit in front of him had become a blur as Abreu continued to scan for missiles.

The radio came to life, startling Abreu.

I'm hit, I'm hit!

The radar was useless; targets continued to appear and disappeared, sometimes as small circles, others as streaks and lines.

It's a trap! Abreu heard another voice.

Mariano, we need to get out of here, his friend's voice called on his radio.

The two Mig-29s continued their climb leaving below a sky glowing bright among the darkness. Abreu glanced down and was shocked at all the explosions happening below them.

Once again he glanced at the radar, which was now a large blob of light. *It wasn't a malfunction,* he thought. *They're jamming us.*

Again the missile alarm began to sound. Abreu immediately fired his countermeasures and moved the stick to his right, feeling the pressure of the G's against his body. Finally, he began to breathe easier as the missile alarm died down.

The radio chatter was almost impossible to understand. There were screams and cries from almost everyone. Some of the fighters tried to descend, only to find American warships waiting for them, their weapons automatically firing at the low flying targets. The ships missiles were also finding easy targets, as a group of ships from the *Washington* Strike Group caught the Cuban fighters unexpectedly.

Some of the fighters tried to fly through the ship gauntlet, only to be met by squadrons of Navy and Air Force fighters coming to intercept them. *Washington* and *Enterprise's* fighters, coming from the east, soon joined the hunt.

The explosion in front of him was sudden and unexpected. Abreu thought the threat had been left behind as he and his friend turned southwest, away from the enemy who had been expecting them all along.

There was no alarm, no trail, only an explosion in front of him, which almost blinded him. As his eyes recovered, Abreu realized that he was alone.

"Berto," he said softly as the darkness returned around him.

Abreu pushed his plane, feeling the effect immediately against his body. In the distance, the flashes seemed faint, almost unreal. It was hard to imagine that minutes ago those men, now disappearing in a blink of an eye, were all joined together in one brave mission. Hard to believe that those flashes were once comrades, friends, husbands, fathers.

The alarm began once again but this time it changed almost immediately. The 'missile lock' alarm changed almost immediately to a more urgent alarm. He was no longer being scanned; the missile was coming for him.

Abreu flew his plane straight, making no sudden move, knowing that soon the missile will find him. There was no escape, no reason to run; there wasn't even a reason to pray, he never believed in God.

Abreu closed his eyes and waited for the inevitable.

Chapter 39

==================

The base was quiet, not unlike any other night. Guards moved about their posts, most of the installation was dark and silent.

The situation was different in other parts of the base. The high school was buzzing with activity as soldiers prepared the area for the oncoming attack. Everyone had been given strict instructions not to be loud. The instruction was not necessary; everyone worked diligently alone with their thoughts.

The capture, or rather, the neutralizing of the two Cuban teams assured everyone that the attack was imminent, and the night was still hiding many more surprises.

All non-essential personnel were long gone and safe somewhere in the states; the rest were too busy concentrating on any small task to keep their mind occupied from the waiting. The local high school, being close to the northeast entrance, had become a small weapons depot assuring that all soldiers were well equipped before the attack.

Admiral Robert Daniels stood next to the counter of the base's McDonald's studying the map as Captain Mendez continued his briefing. Mendez had gone over the information twice before but Daniels felt that the young man was keeping himself busy in the best way he could.

Daniels noticed the edginess on one of his commanders. As head of GiTMO's Joint Task Force, Major General Charles Mendelson's duty was to stop all aggression against the base, and yet he was forced to sit and wait as the Cuban prepared for an attack.

Daniels approached him and stood next to him. "Don't worry Charles."

Mendelson shook his head slightly, still looking forward. "I'm not worried; we are prepared; although a bit restless."

"It's understandable, it's not everyday you prepare for an attack like this one."

"Casualties," Mendelson said. "There will be casualties."

"There usually are."

"Could be avoided," his voice was dry and raspy. "We could attack first."

Daniels turned and noticed Mendelson's look his eyes fixed, his mind going through all the possibilities and scenarios again and again.

"That might be true; but not in the eyes of the world."

Mendelson blinked.

"For years this regime has played games with us. Castro alone has escaped countless of assassination attempts. An unprovoked attack, and believe me he will call it that, will be seen as another attempt of the US—"

"I know the reasons," Mendelson interrupted. "Doesn't change the facts."

The two men stood side-by-side not speaking. Daniels knew that Mendelson was right, but politics always played a bigger role regardless of the amount of lives lost in the process. Cuba could attack but if the US would attack first, it will be seen as a bully, trying to force its way into every part of the world. At this time, thousands were protesting their involvement in so many other places in the globe; attacking a small neighbor like Cuba would only make it worse.

And then there was Castro; a man that always knew how to play every card in his hand. Too many times in the past Castro had turned a damaging situation to his advantage, often embarrassing his enemies instead. He had done it enough times that no president ever brought his name in public. Presidents treated him like an annoyance, a brat asking for attention. In private, Cuba was considered a threat and often a danger.

"You know what?" Daniels finally said in a serious tone.

Mendelson finally turned to face him.

"The smell of fries is driving me crazy."

Sergeant Miguel Iglesias thought of pinching himself. A few weeks ago his unit was moving southwest to be part of a large maneuver, a "show of force," in front of the Americans.

Not everyone was invited to this maneuver; in fact some of his friends were not allowed to come, their tanks used by others less experienced.

At the time Iglesias thought it was an unfair practice. After arriving at Oriente, Iglesias realized the reason why some of his friends were not welcome on the trip.

Iglesias noticed the cameras, positioned strategically along the road. These cameras will soon transmit to the entire island, not a parade of tanks along the perimeter of the American base, but rather a victorious attack against the Imperialists.

He felt the power of the T-80 tank as it began to thrust forward, the engine vibrating all around him. Through the road, around the perimeter of the base, his comrades were moving swiftly placing their tanks near the road. The attack will be simultaneous. While T-80's and T72's began their barrage into the base, his unit will storm the gates surprising the Americans who were either sleeping or dozing off in their posts.

They were aware that the Americans had anti-tank weapons, as well as rapid response units, but between the attack from his comrades and his unit storming into the base. The Americans will be disoriented at best. Of course, his commander had assured them that there would be other surprises as well.

Iglesias' tank, the third in a row of twenty, approached slowly toward the northeast gates. He had visited the gates many times before, even serving in one of the guard towers near the area his tank will soon cross to recover the land that belongs to his people.

His eyes closed, Iglesias recalled the entrance, with the big sign above, "Republic of Cuba, Free Territory in America." Iglesias believed this with all the fibers of his body. His country, his beloved land, was the only territory free of Imperialist oppression.

The muffled "thuds" in the distance was a signal to Iglesias, and everyone in his unit that the attack had started. His body tensed as the T-80 began to move faster.

Captain McNeil waited impatiently as his sonar man continued to work furiously. Both *San Juan* and Pasadena were patrolling each side of the base. A third submarine, the USS Connecticut was quietly shadowing an OSA class patrol boat that continued to inch its way to the base.

Aware of the battle currently happening in the Florida Straight, McNeil's attention was concentrating on the other two targets steaming rapidly near his location.

"Bearing 127."

McNeil nodded. The patrol boats were no match for them; and yet they were full of soldiers ready to storm the base.

"Get a solution," he said as his first officer shouted commands behind him.

Chapter 40

========================

Menendez stood watch on the northeast tower, his eyes scanning the enemy base. His legs tremble, partly by the enthusiasm of the moment but mostly due to the vibration of the tanks that were moving around him. The noise of the engines was deafening, yet there seemed to be no activity on the American side.

"Strange," he said out loud noticing that two of the American towers were empty. Menendez could not understand why the area around the gate was now deserted. He trained his binocular across once again. Two trucks sat near the entrance, but no guards were visible. Alarmed, he began to look, moving frantically trying to find someone. His hand reached for his radio, the fingers almost pressing the button when he stopped himself.

Fifty yards from one of the American sentry tower, almost invisible in the dark, Menendez noticed the small attack buggy. Inside a young Marine sat talking to another soldier. The conversation seemed casual, the Marine in the buggy was laughing.

Menendez felt his breathing returning to normal, his mind no longer warning him of danger. Suddenly, the world around him exploded as the tanks around the perimeter began to fire.

The first T-80 crashed through the gates of the American base and turned left immediately, allowing for the second tank to have a clear shot if it was required. The Marines in the attack buggy near the tower seemed slow in their reaction. Instead of starting the engine, one picked up a small box next to him while the second pulled what seemed to be long tube.

The second tank, still moving through the gates turned its attention to the parked buggy, the torrent moving in their direction. The two trucks parked near the entrance exploded, paralyzing the tank in its tracks. Fire engulfed the inside of the tank and rapidly reaching the ordinance. The third tank, unable to stop fast enough, rammed against the second one. The ordinance of the second tank exploded, damaging the third tank and paralyzing the column of tank behind them.

The fate of the first tank ended as quickly. In the confusion, the crew of the first tank failed to notice the missile from a shoulder mounted antitank system penetrating its armored hull.

Within seconds, the invading forced was paralyzed in the front of the base they were trying to capture.

The tank column, after releasing their first volley began to hear the communication from the invading force. The exhilaration of the attack suddenly became fear. Something was wrong.

The men inside tank #23 worked furiously trying to get the next shell inside when the explosion rocked their tank.

"What was that? What was that?" the shouts began.

Outside, a roar was heard from above, followed by another, as explosions continued to rock the tank.

Tank #23 fired its last volley before it became engulfed in fire.

Menendez opened his eyes touching the blood oozing from the cut on his head. He could not figure out what had happened, for a moment he thought the tower had collapsed and he had lost consciousness.

The explosions were not coming from the American base, but rather from behind the tower. Menendez stumbled to get up, finally looking at the strange noise that was approaching. The sight made him tremble in fear.

"Those are fighters!" he shouted.

He moved slightly to the side, looking at the monitor screen showing the base in front. A building seemed to be on fire as the glow almost blanked out the screen. Through the light he noticed a shadow flying low above the fire. The shadow became two, then three, each becoming larger as they approached his tower.

Three Apache helicopters separated, each firing at a different tank, ignoring Menendez who cursed and shouted at them.

Menendez' legs gave up from under him and he collapse to the ground, his eyes now swelling with tears. "They knew!" he muttered. "They knew we were coming."

Lieutenant Chen veered his F-15 back toward the base. One of the first priorities for the fighters was to protect Leeward Field from any attack. The runway was needed to allow all the fighters to take off.

Chen checked his instruments as the threat indicator began to show the ground targets.

"You got to be kidding me," he said almost smiling.

Ahead, the tanks were lined up around the perimeter road of the base, their turret facing the base as they prepared for another attack.

Chen wondered if he should call in and tell them not to bother with the smart bombs. There was no way to miss this targets that were neither moving nor hidden in any way.

Saying a small prayer, Chen fired his first bomb at the large row of tanks below him.

"We have three more F-15's taking off, as well as two more Apaches." A young lieutenant shouted from the radio. "Confirmed, all Apaches are airborne, two more F-15s are taxiing out."

Daniels was pleased; so far the attack was directed to the barracks and the command buildings, all of them now empty. The decision to move their headquarters to the civilian installation had paid off.

"Only six Cuban attack helicopters crossed to the base. The other eight were destroyed before taking off. I guess they waited too long to use their gunships."

"Very well," Daniels said.

Mendelson approached him, his face still serious. "We have all our tanks moving to intercept. At this point only one of their tanks entered the base but was destroyed immediately."

Daniels seemed please.

"You were right, Camp Delta was one of their targets; most of their gunships were destroyed in that vicinity."

"What of the prisoners?"

"I don't know if it was the drugs we pumped through the vents or the talk that CIA guy had with one of their leaders but the camp is quiet."

"Casualties?" Daniels asked.

"Two, so far; but it's too early to tell."

"Very good," Daniels said. "As for their naval attack; their two remaining patrols turned around. I don't think the base is going to change colors any time soon."

"No sir," Mendelson said trying to avoid a smile.

Chapter 41

===================

Trouble! The com-link came to life.

"What is it?" James responded.

Two tanks and two troop carriers filled with Cuban Militia!

James clicked his com-link to advise his second team as the four men burst through the door.

"We're in trouble," one of his men said closing the door.

James was now trying to reach the rest of his team. "Garcia, Anderson; stay out of sight."

There were two short taps on his com-link signaling him that they had acknowledged.

James looked out through one of the small slits of the bunker. "Hawk?"

All stopped on dirt road; stand by.

James cursed.

General Antonio Guerra scanned the area around the bunker. *There might be no reason to be suspicious,* he thought. It was common for the telephone lines to go dead on different occasions but he needed to be sure. He was now cursing himself for leaving the men alone but his orders were clear: the site should look deserted.

He was still early; after all, the attack on the base would not start for another 30 minutes. That is if Colonel Chavez could follow orders, something Guerra knew the colonel could not do. Whoever put Chavez in charge was taking a great risk. Yet, Guerra had bigger problems; none of his men seemed to be in their posts.

He signaled for the rest of the team to remain by the road as his transport began to move closer to the bunker.

You got eight Militias moving for the door! The com-link came to life once again.

James pulled a small transmitter from his pocket and pressed the button, his team preparing for the door to open.

The explosion threw Guerra to the ground as the area around the second transport and tanks exploded. His ears, still deafened from the sound began to register muffled sounds coming from the bunker. In turn, his eyes watched one of his soldiers falling to the ground.

He turned to give an order but realized that one of his tanks was already moving for the attack. The second tank was partially operational, able to move the turret but unable to move forward due to the explosion.

Guerra ran behind the first tank before it made the turn to the bunker trying to stop it. The driver, seeing his commander running stopped immediately.

"Stay here!" he yelled. "It might be a trap!" The turret of the tank began to swivel as Guerra continued to bark orders from behind. "Avoid the missiles! Avoid the missiles!" he shouted again and again.

"Talk to me Hawk," James called on the radio.

Not good! You took care of the two transports and everyone inside it however the tanks are still operational.

"Damn!" James cursed

Correction, one tank. The other one seems to be stopped, and does not have a clear shot to the bunker.

"Could this thing hold an attack?" Garcia asked jumping down from the roof access, quickly followed by Anderson.

Incoming!

The thunderous noise made their teeth rattle as the ground shook from under them. Dust filled the bunker as a few rocks fell around them.

"Good old Soviet technology," someone shouted.

"Are you referring to the bunker or the tank? Anderson asked.

"Hawk?" James called his sniper once again.

You got some damage, a few more hits and you guys are done. Hawk replied watching the scene unfold in front of him.

A sudden noise startled him as the second tank opened fire. The shot missed the bunker entirely exploding in the sugar cane field.

"The other tank has joined the party," Hawk called to James.

"You idiot!" Guerra shouted running to the second tank in anger. In two bounds he reached the top and threw the hatch open.

The men inside the tank turned alarmed, seeing their commanding officer, his gun pointing at them.

"Don't shoot!" he screamed once again.

Slightly ahead, tank number one fired once again.

The second hit took a large piece of roof. The bunker began to give in.

"One more shot and we're done." Garcia said.

James looked around and gave the order. "Everyone, up on the roof. We'll jump down and try to make a run to the field.

The order wasn't finished when most of them were on their way up.

"Hawk, we're going to need some cover." James knew the request was useless. The answer on his com-link was immediate.

Moving for a shot on their commander.

James reached the roof and counted his blessing. The attack had knocked out the two large floodlights leaving the camp in darkness. He moved his night-vision goggles down and ran to the northwest side of the roof. What he saw did not make him feel better. The northwest part of the field registered immediately in his goggles; removing them once again, James noticed the fire nearby.

The explosion behind him threw him to the floor as the building caught another direct hit from the tank. He tried to move up quickly feeling the floor below him beginning to rumble.

James reached for the ledge but the roof collapsed taking him down with it.

Hawk tried unsuccessfully to target the man running back and forth between the two tanks. He had missed the only opportunity he had watching the team make it to safety and shooting a wounded militiaman that was inching toward them.

Noticing James on the roof, Hawk turned his attention back to the man in charge; but he was, again hiding behind one of the tanks.

Hawk noticed the roof collapsing but assumed James was already on the ground. He aimed his scope to the right side of the tank; waiting for the general to make his move.

The sound behind him startled him. He looked back as the distinct sound of machinery continued to approach. Hawk saw a third tank moving in, followed by two more troop transports.

"Captain we have a problem," he called on his com-link.

The response on his ear was silence.

"Captain?" he called again. "Kris!"

The Surface-To-Air missile attack from the island was becoming a headache for the planes and ships in the Straight of Florida. The missiles were older, slow moving rockets, most lacking targeting and range. That was the main problem.

The lack of range made the missiles more dangerous to the ships than the planes. The fleet was prepared for multiple waves of fighters as well as a barrage of missiles. What nobody was expecting was the antiquated missiles that were now falling from the sky, their fuel consumed in a futile attempt to reach a target.

Both vessels and fighters continue the hunt for missiles some of which were falling too close to the Strike Group. Any hit by the missiles would be attributed more to luck than to targeting. Still, the nuisance of these missiles was making it harder to detect the real threat.

The Missile Cruiser *Gettysburg* slowly moved away from the rest of the group, preparing for the new mission at hand.

"Sir, a new wave of fighters is taking off from the island," Gettysburg radioman announced.

Captain Norris paid no attention, his orders were clear.

Gettysburg moved into position, its cargo ready for deployment.

"Sir coordinates entered; missiles ready."

The captain could not hide his troubled look.

"Sir?" the young man called again.

Norris knew what he must do. It didn't matter that the young man ready to fire the two Tomahawk missiles arrived only a few hours ago with the man now standing next to him. It didn't matter that the two missiles, ready to leave his ship were not part of the original ordinance; nor that they did not look like regular Tomahawks.

Captain Norris only knew one thing, the fact that he still had to give the order.

Van Buren's voice was soft and understanding. "Captain, if you please."

Captain Norris closed his eyes and gave the command. He knew the consequences of his action, but he also recognized that it was an order he had to obey.

Chapter 42

==================

Maldonado put the receiver down slowly, his face in shock, his hands trembling.

"Our planes were intercepted by American ships and planes off the coast of Florida, among them the USS Enterprise."

Fidel Castro remained unmoved, ignoring his brother now collapsed on the chair next to the large oak desk.

"Not one single plane reached its target."

Raul bit his lip. "How could they've known?"

"It gets worse," Maldonado said. "Our attack on Guantanamo faired no better. The Americans were waiting with planes, helicopters and tanks of their own."

"How could they've known?" Raul continued to repeat.

"Any tanks reached the inside of the base?"

"I don't have much information, but one was destroyed inside while another was stopped at the doors."

"Two!" Castro seemed pleased. "We had our troops inside the base."

"They knew!" Raul cried out.

"Of course they did," Fidel said. "Did you actually expect this attack to succeed?"

"Sir?" Maldonado looked stunned. "What are you saying?"

"This was not about destroying the base; in fact attacking Guantanamo was only a diversion. The true target has always been Miami." Castro tried to stand up but couldn't. He frowned and tried once again.

Maldonado picked up the phone to make a call. "The word is getting around; soon things will get out of hand. We have to get out of here as soon as possible."

Again, Fidel tried to get up from the chair. "That explains it," he said. "You knew I would refuse to leave. You drugged me!" His eyes were fixed on his brother, the disappointment was clear.

"I'm sorry, my brother. You have to survive, the Revolution—"

"The Revolution?" Castro said tying to keep his eyes from closing. "I am the Revolution. I alone can say when the Revolution is over."

"The plane's ready," Maldonado said, hanging up the phone.

"We'll never make it," Fidel whispered. "One of the missiles' targets is the Nuclear Power Plant in Miami. The other…" Fidel tried to maintain awake. "The second will hit Habana almost immediately."

"What!?!" the two men turned.

"It is so clear now, my brother." Castro said between breaths. "The Revolution was about struggle, about fighting against all the odds. It was never about ruling or being the head of a government."

The two men approached Fidel who had become silent. They tried to grab him but he began again.

"That is the legacy I will leave all Cubans. They will have to continue the struggle, they will never stop fighting—"

"Grab him while I get help," Raul said. As long as Guerra doesn't get that phone call, we can get out of here."

"—and a nuclear explosion in Habana; only one country could've done that." Fidel was almost out of breath now, a smile almost visible. "The Americans will be blamed."

"Kris!" Hawk called again not caring if his voice was heard below.

The static in his com-link continued.

Hawk aimed his gun at the man who continued to run around giving orders. "You're dead, you son of a bitch!"

Guerra commanded his tank crew to stop firing as the corner of the bunker collapse. He remained behind the tank covering himself from any Americans who tried to attack.

Although there didn't seem to be any activity since his soldiers were killed in front of the door, Guerra remained cautious. The attack was quick and precise, something that could only have been accomplished by a group of US commando.

How they found the location was unimportant, Guerra knew that they would be dead soon enough. From the corner of his eye he noticed something and he turned; smiling when he saw the troop transports edge its way down.

The terrain was steep as the transport stopped a few feet behind the burned truck blocking the way. The soldiers moved swiftly out of the truck and next to their commanding officer.

Guerra remained smiling realizing that the annoyance would soon be put away. He looked at his watch knowing that soon the missiles would need to be readied. The bunker was not needed; the trucks carrying the missiles were completely self-sufficient, with all the necessary equipment to send them to their target.

The Special Edition Mercedes Limo raced through the streets of Havana. Traffic was light at this time and Maldonado was in too much of a hurry to wait for any security. The plane was waiting and only three passengers would be leaving, there was no need for anyone else; not even a pilot.

"It's too late," Fidel whispered from the back seat, his hand holding a cellular phone. "I just made the call."

Maldonado watched through the rear view mirror as his supreme leader collapse once again, a cell phone dropping from his hand.

The shot hit Guerra on the shoulder and spun him around. Falling on his back, he tried to get up but felt a sharp pain from his shoulder all the way down his spine. His soldiers were crouched behind the tank as Guerra tried to figure out where the shot came from.

Sniper, he thought. *I forgot the sniper.*

He bit his lip hard, trying to get up once again, his teeth breaking the skin of his lip. The pain was unbearable and Guerra felt back, paralyzed.

Closing his eyes, he tried to summon enough willpower to force himself up. The ringing around him continued making Guerra realize that it was coming from his uniform. "The call," he whispered. "We have to fire the missiles."

One of his soldiers moved closer, trying to understand what he was saying.

Guerra began to speak again, he needed to order his men to prepare the missiles; it was the only thing that mattered.

The darkness of the sky seemed to grow into large wings, reaching out for him. Guerra blinked watching the wings spread apart, showing a creature now growing larger, moving ever so closely.

The soldiers next to him moved back confused as Guerra screamed in horror, his eyes fixed into the night sky.

Like in his nightmare, when he was just a child, the large bat-like creature came screeching towards him. He saw the beast even closer, his mouth opening to show its large fangs. Guerra blinked trying to focus, watching the fangs separating from the beast and reaching out for him.

The fighting lasted no more than 30 minutes, a time that seemed like an eternity to some. Daniels, not moving from the window continued to watch the small fires in the distance.

"We had some casualties," Mendelson said. "Overall, I think we did better than expected."

Daniels nodded. "It wasn't so much that we were ready, but rather the fact that they didn't put up too much of a fight."

"Those poor bastards, they knew this battle was useless. Even so, they follow their orders blindly."

"You do, when that is all you know." Daniels turned back from the window, the first time since the attack started. "What's our status?"

"Some of the buildings were hit hard but we can repair them. The biggest problem—"

The noise was unbearable, making both Daniels and Mendelson cover their ears. As the men turned, an explosion rocked the area throwing them back.

"What the hell was that?" Daniels said; his body covered in glass from the shattered window.

Chapter 43

==================

The exploding tank startled Hawk who was aiming for another soldier. "What the—?"

Captain James, this is Black-Wing 2; please respond.

Another explosion shot dirt past Hawk.

"Black Wing 2, this is Lieutenant Randall."

Lieutenant Randall, what's your situation?

Hawk turned his attention to the area where the tanks once stood. Twisted metal was all that remained. Above, the silhouette of two F-117, Stealth Fighters disappeared back into the night's sky.

"You guys took care of our little problem. Thank you."

Roger that. *We'll just keep you cover until your transport arrives.*

Hawk heard the chatter on the radio as the rest of the team began to reappear. He smiled and called for Garcia. "Area secure, let's get back to those missiles."

On it, Garcia replied.

'Hawk' Randall never radioed what he was thinking; he knew that Garcia was already sending someone to search for Captain James.

Commander Williams' mission was only to patrol the western side of the island. As *Enterprise* and *Washington*'s air wing continue to patrol the 'no fly zone' between the island and Miami, Williams and his wingman were now moving away from the action. Although the entire attack began in the north side of the island, command was still concerned that forces could be gathering in other areas.

Williams knew that they would be in constant contact with both the Sentry, watching the skies over the island, and USS Washington. He wasn't worried about losing communications nor was he worried about fighter attacks. The events hours ago proved that the Cubans MiGs were easily outmaneuvered and outgunned.

"Foxtrot 2, this is Foxtrot 1," Williams said through his mask.

On your six, boss, his wingman replied immediately.

"I'm reading a bogey, dead ahead."

Roger, it just took off.

"Let's investigate."

The two F-18s hit the afterburners simultaneously and accelerated across the island.

The small Russian-made passenger plane rose swiftly and steadied on its course south. Maldonado, piloting the plane, had no intention on waiting for the fighter escort. "They can catch up," he said, holding the controls tightly.

The American fighters were busy with the new missile, and fighter threat, on the Florida Straight to be bothering with a small, unarmed plane.

Maldonado smiled at the sight of the three MIG-29s now joining his aircraft.

"Three more bogies," Williams announced on the radio.

Roger that. Whoever is in that plane is getting some serious protection.

"Let's take care of that escort before we find out who that is." Williams armed his Hornet, preparing himself as well for the impending attack.

According to MIG #2, the closest threat was roughly 100 kilometers away and at the time posing no threat. The error proved costly as MIG #2 exploded. The plane dropped behind slightly to ensure that the two fast moving targets were not part of a larger group. The pilot ensured his comrade that he could take care of two American fighters. Ignoring his plane's missile warning, the pilot continued on a path to intercept thinking that the American planes were still too far to fire, not realizing that the distance was within the range of the oncoming Phoenix missile.

The remaining two MiGs turned to intercept the two intruders leaving the small plane to continue its escape from the island.

The MiGs were prepared for the attack, but they would not reach missile lock for another 20 kilometers. In return, three AIM-120C-5 missiles began an intercept course from the American fighters.

MIG #1 avoided the first missile while moving closer for a lock. In contrast, MIG #3 disappeared from his radar; two "Slammers" exploding around it.

Panicking, the pilot of MIG #1, still without a lock, fired a spread of missiles at the upcoming fighters. Seconds later, his planes burst into flame from a new Air-To-Air missile.

Conner had followed the action from the situation room in the Homestead Air Reserve Base. The missile attack was already dying down, most of them falling into the ocean without causing any damage.

The fighter attack was suppressed almost immediately, not allowing a single MiG to cross the American gauntlet. The missile attack however proved to be a logistic headache since most were crashing into the sea, their fuel exhausted. The early demise of the missile and their unusual slow speed created trouble for some of the fighters.

Two of the remaining Cuban MiGs used this second wave to their advantage, sneaking away on an attack course to the Florida Keys. Their move did not go unnoticed as fighters from the Boca Chica Naval Base moved immediately to intercept.

The Cuban pilots, knowing their impending doom, fired their ordinance at the stretch of land ahead of them.

Damage report from Key West was now arriving at Homestead. Buildings in the southernmost city of the United State were in flames.

Conner's attention however was now turned to his cell phone.

"Yes sir," he replied. His face was suddenly serious. He tried to hide the look but Becker immediately noticed.

"I understand sir."

Becker stood next to him waiting for the end of the call.

"Yes, sir. Thank you."

Conner pressed the 'end' button and put his cellular phone away.

"Van Buren?" Becker asked.

"Yup," Conner said turning away from her.

"What is it?"

"Gitmo got a few hits, nothing major. The attack is over."

"That's good news," she said waiting for more.

"Camp Delta received a direct hit from some kind of missile. The entire camp was destroyed."

"The prisoners?"

Conner shook head, turning once again away from Becker.

She did not ask any other question. She knew there was something else; something Van Buren told Conner. Whatever it was, it will remain between them, and whoever else was involved. She moved closer and hugged him, feeling his arm holding her tight.

Williams threw the helmet down hard cursing again. "Stupid!"

He was so sure that the two missiles would take care of the MiGs; he immediately began to concentrate on the civilian airplane before the missiles hit their target.

The MIG responded with a missile attack of its own; one that Williams was too slow or too 'stupid' to react to.

The Russian made missile clipped the right wing of his Hornet forcing him to parachute down to the island. Moments later his F-18 exploded against a mountain a few miles ahead. During his descend; Williams saw the small executive plane spiraling out of control, the victim of one of his missiles that missed the original target.

"I'm probably the only pilot shot down today," he muttered to himself. He could see the grin in Moore's face; his wingman took care of all three MiGs.

"Stupid!"

The wing of the Russian private plane ended over three hundred yards ahead of the wreckage. Not far from it, the motionless body of Maldonado remained unmoved.

Fidel Castro opened his eyes, his body sore, his leg covered in blood. He tried to wake his brother but he soon realized that the man was no longer breathing.

The door gave in to his weight and he tumbled out of the plane. He tried to get up but fell to his side as his leg gave way beneath him. Castro reached for it, touching it; he realized that it was probably broken. His mind still disoriented from the crash, and the drugs.

Castro closed his eyes, willing all the pain away, trying to focus on the current task. *Get up!* He shouted to himself.

He opened his eyes noticing a pair of feet near him. He turned to notice that a group of 'campesinos' had gathered near the wreck, all eyes now focused on him.

With a grunt he managed to get to his feet. Straightening his uniform, he stood tall and strong, even the pain seemed to disappear. He felt his power reaching out for the crowd that continued to grow, their faces showing the fear for the man, *no*, he thought, *the god,* standing in front of them.

He took a small step forward as the crowd moved back.

"Compañeros," he said finally.

The crowd stood motionless, the sound of their breathing their only response.

"Comrades,' he said firmly.

A small pebble flew from within the crowd and struck him on the center of the uniform, falling to the ground as he watched the crowd move away from the person responsible.

A small child, roughly 6 or 7 picked up another pebble and threw it at him once again. His face showed no fear at the man in front of him.

Castro wasn't amused. "Come here!" he said with an angry voice.

The little boy picked up a larger rock and threw it, this time trying to hit Castro on the face.

The rock flew past Castro's face, and struck the fuselage of the plane behind him.

Castro's anger was now obvious, seeing the kid reaching out for another.

The pain was immediate as another rock hit Castro on the head. The new rock did not come from the kid this time. Castro turned, noticing a woman reaching out for a rock.

Behind her, an old man, barely able to stand was raising a stick and screaming at him.

"Hermanos!" he shouted. But his brothers were no longer listening. Each hand in the crowd began to reach for a weapon, their faces desperate to be the one to destroy the monster in front of them.

Epilogue

===========

Conner sat on the floor, his shirt drenched in sweat as he struggled to catch his breath.

"I believe that's game," James said limping to the back.

"You're limping again," Conner said. "I thought you were completely recovered."

"I kicked your ass, didn't I?"

Conner nodded struggling to get up. He walked slowly to his gym bag and picked up a towel. "That was some job you guys did."

"Bull!" James replied. "If you wouldn't have sent those fighters—"

"I don't know what you're talking about." Conner said hiding a smile.

James was serious, his eyes looking at Conner intensely. "No, I mean it. Thanks."

"Don't mention it."

"The guys wanted to take you out for drinks or something," James said uncomfortably.

"It's not necessary," Conner said going back to his bag. "But you have my number." He picked up a box and handed it to James. "No music, no press, no fanfare; you know the drill."

"My men deserve it better than I do."

"They are all getting one." Conner interrupted. "I have them in the car; I thought you might want to give it to them. You know, however you guys handle this."

"Thanks," James said shaking his hand. "I hear congratulations are in order for you,"

"Maybe. There will be a hearing soon. Congress wants to investigate how much we knew about this attack. There's also the question of the destruction of Camp Delta and the death of all those prisoners."

James nodded. "Well, for what it's worth, congratulations."

The two men reached Conner's car. Without a word Conner opened the trunk and retrieved a box. "Wish we could make this public."

"Nah, we like it this way." James said taking the box from him. "The guys owe you and they definitely want to meet you."

"Call me. I'd like to meet them as well." Conner said getting in his car.

The racquetball game had taken the edginess he was feeling. For almost three days Conner felt nervous, anxious, worrying too much about the meeting today. Now that the day was here, he knew that he had no choice than to finally confront the man. In an hour Steven Conner was finally meeting his destiny, the man that he would soon call, 'father-in-law.'

The area was quiet, and deserted. It was the perfect setting, the way he preferred it.

Both Conner and Henderson offered to drive him here, but he preferred to be here by himself. It was the way he worked, the way he lived, his way.

Juan Navarro kneeled by the grave of Maria Cecilia Fernandez, not looking at the tombstone, or the empty plastic base on the corner. Placing a lonely white rose on the ground, he touched marble slab finally, wishing it were her face, at least one more time.

Conner told him that every war had its martyrs, and Marcie was truly the one here.

"Hi baby," he finally said. "You finally made it to the United States."

- 200 -

He could not help but smile when his first, lonely tear, was brushed away as a gentle breeze softly touched him on the face.

The End

www.ingramcontent.com/pod-product-compliance
Lightning Source LLC
Chambersburg PA
CBHW031309280626
47169CB00017B/1081